Shameless

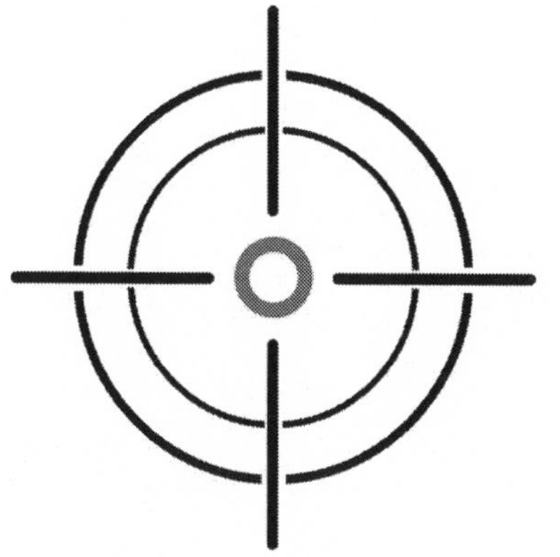

the Shameless trilogy

Shameless
Shameful
UnAshamed

Shameless

M. MALONE
NANA MALONE

MALONE^2
SQUARED

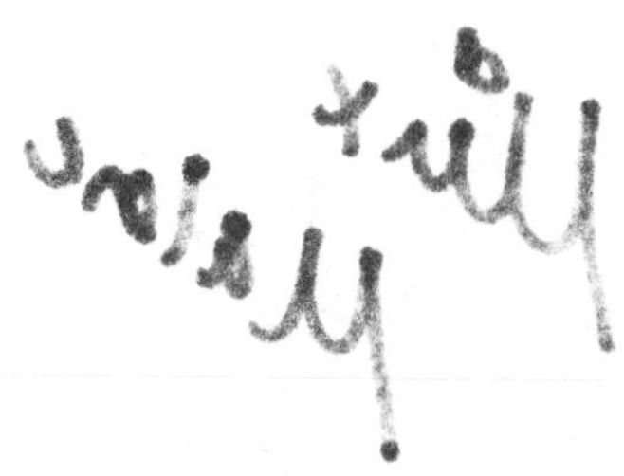

Shameless

A MALONE SQUARED PUBLICATION

For information address:
MALONE SQUARED, 340 S Lemon Ave #9016, Walnut , CA 91789

ISBN-10: 1-946961-01-9
ISBN-13: 978-1-946961-01-3

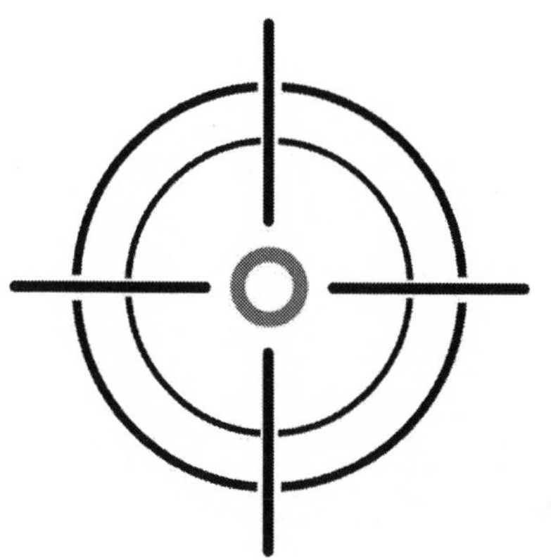

Chapter One

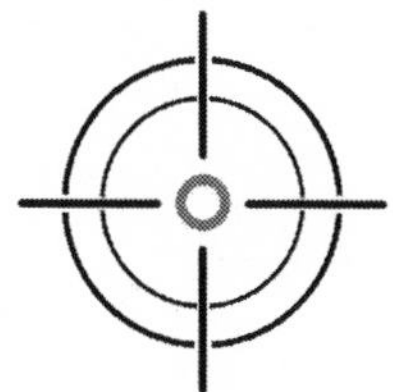

There was nothing like the sound of New York City in the morning.

Between the honking cars, the cursing and the never-ending rush of voices, just walking down the street was an assault to the senses. To everyone else it sounded like noise but to Lucia DeMarco it was a raw kind of symphony. It was a reminder that despite everything she'd been through, she was still here.

She was still here and *still* late.

Already she was out of breath as she hurried across the street, narrowly missing being hit by yet *another* cab. Unfortunately, Lucia didn't do the delicate, charmingly breathless thing. Oh no. Sweating caused her overly curly hair to stick to her forehead like stringy noodles and she didn't pant for air in a sexy, Marilyn Monroe kind of way, either. Instead it was more like gasping out her last breath. Her job as a fashion assistant for THE up and coming fashion line didn't leave much time for anything unnecessary like sleeping, eating or going to the gym. She made a mental note to start taking better care of herself and filed it along with the ten thousand other things she did not have time for.

Dodging traffic counted as a workout, right?

Her phone vibrated in the pocket of her skirt, the early morning humidity and her sweat already making the fabric stick to her legs. She pulled it out while trying to balance the tray of coffees she held with her other arm. Her handbag, a sample from a new designer that her friend JJ had given her just last week, banged against her hip as she trotted through the crosswalk while reading her phone.

- Where the hell are you? Adriana is losing her shit!

Lucia groaned and walked faster. It had taken her longer than expected to get the coffee and she was cutting it way too close to being subject to one of Adriana's famous tirades. If she'd known she'd be running across town perhaps she would have worn something other than four - inch heels. Perhaps the adorable ballet flats she'd borrowed from the sample closet just last night. However, this was the only chance she'd have to stop by the records office today so she'd have to ignore her already throbbing feet.

When the records office in Southampton had told her they'd sent some of their archives to be held in the city, she'd assumed her research had hit a dead end. It had taken her years to piece together the information she had, and it had been a long shot anyway. After all, what did she expect? Lucia gulped down the huge knot that always rose in her throat when she thought about her brother. Rafe had been gone for six years now, and there were still days she woke up thinking she was fifteen years old again and her favorite person in the world would be in the kitchen making her pancakes.

It was a knife to the gut every time her mind cleared and she remembered that he was gone.

The details of that day were still not entirely clear, but she'd managed to piece together where the shooting had taken place and had used every spare moment over the past year to find out more about the owners of the property. It was a struggle to find anyone who remembered anything about it, which was strange in a town where everyone knew everyone. But her tenacity had paid off because she'd gotten a name and had looked up the deed. It had been sold multiple times since then, and the local records office had only digitized their files the prior year. Somehow, some of the files related to the property had been sent off to archives accidentally.

Lucia looked up at the sign over the drab gray building that housed the New York State archives. Her heartbeat danced in her chest. Whatever she found out today could either shed light on the worst day of her life or lead to another dead end. The heavy glass door opened and as she tried to move out of the way, the coffee tray tilted slightly, leaving a wet, brown spot on the front of her white silk blouse. *Awesome*. There was no way Adriana would miss that.

"Sorry!"

She nodded absently as the man who'd been in such a hurry continued down the sidewalk without taking a second glance back.

"Good day to you, too."

She pulled the door open and let out a sigh of relief when she saw there was no one else inside. The gods of karma were taking pity on her finally.

"Hi, Brent. I got your message that you have something for me?"

The man behind the counter glanced up from his computer and smiled. Average height with dark hair and a nice smile, Brent was a nice guy. *Nice* seemed to be the only word she could think of to describe him, actually. He'd helped her fill out an official request the last time she was there and had promised to look in the archives personally. The fact that he'd flirted with her made her feel a little guilty. Lucia had never been the bat-your-eyelashes type and she had no plans to start now. However, she was willing to take any help she could get at this point.

"Hi, how's your day going so far?"

Lucia set the tray of coffee on the counter between them and hitched her bag higher on her shoulder. She gestured at the brown stain and grinned. "Amazing! As you can see."

He chuckled, although his eyes lingered on the swell of her breasts a bit longer than was strictly polite. Lucia cleared her throat and his eyes finally snapped back up to hers.

"You said you found something?" she prodded.

"I did. Sorry it took me so long. I'm not sure what happened when the files were transferred, but a bunch of files were in the wrong boxes. Though, as luck would have it, I finally found the deed of sale from the time period you asked for. I made a copy of it for you."

He reached under the counter and pulled out a yellow, legal-size envelope. With shaking fingers, Lucia pulled it across the counter toward her. She lifted the flap with the tip of her index finger but then closed it again. Tonight was soon enough to go down that rabbit hole.

"So, I was wondering if, maybe, I mean you might not be into it…"

Her phone buzzed in her pocket again and Lucia pulled it out, smiling apologetically at Brent who didn't even notice. She glanced down at the text message from JJ. It was marked as *Urgent*.

- Remember that painting on the wall of Rocco's when we were there for dinner last week? Adriana wants a swatch of

Belgian linen in the exact same shade.

Lucia glanced up at Brent, who was still droning on, before quickly typing an answer.

- Belgian Linen in a shade of blue that I barely remember. That's it? You can't tell me anything else?

- You know how she is. Just get back here. Fast!

After stashing her phone back in her pocket, Lucia picked up the envelope and threw it in her bag. It was only when she looked up again that she realized Brent was staring at her.

"So, what do you think?" he asked.

"Um, sounds good?" Lucia had no idea what he'd been talking about and then instantly felt guilty for not listening, especially after he'd been so helpful. But she had to magically cross town in less than ten minutes and also conjure up a fabric that looked like something her boss had seen in a restaurant last week.

"I hate to cut and run but I'm late. So, I guess I'll see you later." She picked up the tray of coffee, wondering if she should take it back to the office before going back out for the linen swatches.

"Really?" Brent clapped his hands, the loud sound startling her so badly she almost dropped the coffee entirely. He ran a hand through his hair and let out a loud sigh as if he'd just run a marathon. "I mean, that's great. I've been wanting to try this place for a while and I think you'll really like it. So I'll pick you up at seven, if that's okay?"

Wait, what?

Lucia laughed nervously when she realized exactly

what she'd missed while engrossed in her phone. She forced a smile while Brent opened a new contact on his phone and then typed her number in. A minute later she was outside on the sidewalk with cold coffee and a date.

It wasn't the worst thing ever, to go out with a nice guy. Although, she had a feeling Noah wouldn't feel that way when he found out. She winced, imagining how that would go over. But he wasn't her daddy or her brother. Just a family friend who was way too bossy for his own good. Maybe she wouldn't tell him. Or she could text him. He couldn't yell at her over text message.

Nonna had always said that technology would be the death of communication.

"How do you want to play this?"

Noah Blake tugged the baseball cap he wore lower over his forehead before responding to the voice coming through his earpiece. "The usual. Unless he refuses our invitation."

"You think he'll come easy, mate?"

Matthias, the insanely brilliant and also incredibly annoying tech god that he'd had the good sense to hire/rescue years ago had never been the most optimistic guy. One of the reasons they got along so well.

"Do they ever?"

Noah glanced at the row house across the street currently housing their target, William Chamberlin. There was nothing special about this guy at all, just another asshole who needed a reminder that stalking was illegal. They handled several of these a month, and while they weren't particularly interesting, there was something satisfying about these cases.

Jonas's voice came through his earpiece next. "If he doesn't, then I'll change his mind."

Noah had to smile at the predictable reply. Opening his own security firm had given him financial freedom and the stability he needed after his chaotic early years, but it also brought a world of headaches. Namely, keeping the merry band of past criminals he employed on the straight and narrow.

"Just don't kill him."

Jonas made a sound that could have been a laugh or a snort. "First it was 'don't sleep with the clients.' Now you're telling me I can't kill people? You're no fun lately."

"When has he ever been fun?" Matthias interjected.

That actually made Noah smile. If someone had told him years ago that he'd be the voice of reason, hell, the responsible one, he'd have thought they were on something. But that was before Rafe died.

That was before Lucia.

Thoughts of her always carried a range of emotions

from protectiveness to desire, and of course, there was the guilt. Always the damn guilt. Noah shook his head. He'd promised Rafe that he'd look after her, and he'd done that. It was the least he could do for the man who'd pulled him out of the gutter and shown him a better way to live. He'd upheld his oath and honored the memory of his best friend every day.

But while he'd done his best to shelter her over the past few years, he could never truly be honest with her. She'd never look at him the same way if she knew what he was truly capable of. What her beloved brother had been capable of. It was a quandary with no solution. There was nothing he could do about that. So he'd keep doing what he did best… *Lie, cheat and kill?* No. Damn it. He shoved the errant thought that slid in on the shoulders of his guilt aside. He would protect her. Just like always.

"Let's get this fucker."

He kept his head down as he approached the building, noting that the street was empty and there was no movement in the house. He knew Jonas would approach from the back to prevent any possibility of the target slipping through their grasp. This was a standard job, just letting the guy know that it was best if he stayed away from their client. He wouldn't call it threatening. Threaten was such a harsh word. This was more like a conversation, but it was a fine line they walked. They did what was necessary to keep their clients safe and most of it was borderline as hell. Just like the rest of his life.

"Guys, we've got a runner. He's going out the back." Matthias sounded as annoyed as Noah felt, his British accent coming across as clipped. Suddenly, he could hear Matthias in his other comm unit, on the secondary channel. "Noah, head's up. Lucia has a date tonight. You want me to do the usual?"

Son of a bitch. If he wasn't chasing assholes, he was making sure some grab-handy dipshit didn't get his grubby little paws on his best friend's little sister.

"Yeah, the usual. I'll get to her as soon as I can." Noah quickened his pace. He could hear the sound of Jonas's breathing in his other earpiece and knew he wasn't in position yet.

"Jonas, he's probably going to cut over to the next street. Go around and cut him off."

"Got it."

He could hear a variety of sounds that were hard to decipher: Jonas's breathing, the clang that could be a metal fence, and then the unmistakable sound of scuffling. A few muffled curses later, it was quiet.

When he rounded the corner, Jonas already had the guy on the ground with one arm twisted behind his back.

"Good work. I didn't really feel like sweating today."

Jonas made a face. "Fuck you, Noah. These shoes were not meant for running."

The guy on the ground craned his neck, trying to see over his shoulder. When he caught sight of Noah, he struggled against Jonas's hold and got a knee in his back for the trouble.

"What the fuck, man? Get off me!"

Noah squatted next to him and then pulled out a small picture of a pretty redhead. Clara Spencer. Although she looked nothing like Lucia, it wasn't a mystery to him why he took these cases so seriously.

Lucia was a good girl; Nonna DeMarco had made sure of that. But even good girls had to grow up some time. And since Rafe wasn't here to protect her like a big brother, Noah would have to do it. There would come a day when Lucia started dating seriously, and just the possibility that one of those fuckers might treat her like this dickhead, terrorizing her with the threat of what he might do, made Noah want to put his fist through a wall…or this douchebag's face.

What if something had happened to him? What if he'd died the same day as Rafe? Lucia might have ended up just like Clara Spencer. There were so many girls out there with no one to stand for them. It was his pleasure to stand for as many of them as he could.

He flipped the photo around. At the sight, William blanched and then started struggling anew. Jonas twisted his arm higher until it was clear that he wasn't going anywhere.

"Do you recognize her? Hmm? I think you do." Noah spoke softly, having learned over the years that a soft voice could often convey menace more convincingly than a loud one.

"No. I've never seen her before!"

"You're a terrible liar, William. Almost as bad as you are at listening. Because Clara has told you several times not to contact her again. Since you didn't seem to be getting the picture, we thought we'd stop by and make sure we're all on the same page."

Casually, Noah reached in his pocket and pulled out an apple. Then his knife. He ignored the other man's whimpers and sliced a bit of skin off the fruit.

"Now there's several ways this can go down. Option number one: You agree to stay away from Clara. My buddy over there—" He pointed at Jonas with the edge of the knife. "—goes home and finishes wanking to Britney Spears videos."

"Fucking hell," Jonas mumbled under his breath. "You know I prefer Christina Aguilera. She is dirty after all."

"And I go home and pretend I didn't spend my morning in the shittiest part of the city waiting on you. But honestly, I'm feeling a little cranky and you don't look that bright. So we're going to stop wasting time and just get on with option number two."

"I didn't do anything, I swear," William mumbled, his face half pressed into the ground.

"I know. And we're going to make sure it stays that way."

Noah sliced off the last bit of skin and then took a bite out of the apple before handing the knife to Jonas.

William let out a low whimper. Once he realized that there was no way to escape Jonas's iron-tight grip, he went slack and a dark spot appeared on the front of his jeans.

Noah sighed. This was about to get messy.

Chapter Two

Noah watched the date from the comfort of his SUV. All the while silently fuming.

What the hell did Lucia think she was doing? His team hadn't vetted the guy. They didn't know anything about him. So far, she'd broken all of the dating rules he'd given her.

For the first date, always meet your date at your designated location. And of course, she'd let this doofus pick her up for their date. As if he hadn't told her a million times to do the exact opposite.

He'd also been very clear not to get in the car with her date. So that was rule one and rule two broken right off the bat. As if he hadn't trained her on how to be careful and what to watch out for. But *oh no*, Lucia didn't listen to shit. Every time he turned around, there she was, careening headfirst into trouble.

Maybe she didn't see her date as a potential threat, but dammit she needed to be more careful. What the hell did she even know about this guy?

"What the hell kind of name is Brent anyway?"

Noah hadn't even realized that he'd spoken out loud, until the voice in his comm unit laughed. "Last I checked, Brent is a perfectly normal name. Lots of guys have it."

Noah barely restrained a growl. "Matthias, when I want your input, I'll give it to you."

There was a chuckle on the other end of the line. Noah made a mental note to give Matthias some really horrible surveillance duty for the next month. This wasn't funny. This was Lucia. They all cared about her well-being.

Maybe you more than the others.

Yeah, so what? He cared about her. And maybe it wasn't the easiest thing in the world watching her date loser after loser. But it was his job, no strike that, it was his *responsibility* to look after her. He owed Rafe that much. But how the hell was he supposed to look out for her when she kept making it so damn difficult? Lucia was obstinate, infuriating, pigheaded, and—

Beautiful.

No. She was like a little sister to him. Yet somehow his dick couldn't seem to get with that program lately. More and more frequently, some very *unsisterly* thoughts wormed their way into his consciousness.

"Matthias, give me something on this Brent guy. Aren't you supposed to be some kind of super-hacker?"

"You better believe it. But, there's nothing on him. Everything is normal. Boring. Most interesting thing about this guy is he likes adventure sports. He skydives, bungee jumps, that sort of thing. Does some triathlons. Maybe he's some kind of adrenaline junkie. But there's nothing else on him. No flags. He lives here in New York in the East Village. No roommates, rent isn't exorbitant. Works for the city. No large withdrawals of cash, good credit. As far as I can tell, he's clean. But that's just his electronic trail. Maybe you're right on this one and he's a little too clean. I mean, there's not even an online dating profile on him. To me, that's weird. Who doesn't have an online dating profile?"

Noah chuckled and then lifted his binoculars again. Lucia was laughing at something. So Brent thought he was a comedian, huh? What the hell was so damn funny? There was too much interference to use the boom mic, otherwise he'd know.

Brent reached across the table and took Lucia's hand, and Noah nearly chipped a tooth from grinding his teeth so hard. He could see Lucia's eyes go wide. Was that surprise? He hoped it was disgust.

Did she actually like this guy?

His gut clenched at the thought. Perfect, just what he needed. Lucia liking this fucking idiot.

It wasn't that she hadn't dated before. She had. Mostly in college. Most of those guys had merely needed a strong reminder to mind their Ps & Qs with her. But this guy, this guy was random—unknown. Which meant it would take more work to scare him off. But Noah was up for the challenge.

Lucia deserved to be happy, just with somebody vetted and approved. After the shit she had survived in her life? The girl needed some happy endings.

Fuck. Not happy endings.

He groaned and turned his attention back to the restaurant. Brent raised a hand and signaled their server. Shit, they were leaving. The real trick was guessing where they were going. He'd put a tracker on her phone, so if he guessed wrong, he could always follow. But what if something happened to her before he could get there?

"Matthias, turn on the listening device on her phone. I'm heading to the house in case that's where they go."

There was a beat of silence. He could almost hear Matthias's silent condemnation. "The thing is, Noah, she's not going to like that."

"The thing is, Matthias, I don't care," he muttered using the same singsong tone.

Yeah, he knew he sounded like an asshole. But this

was Lucia. If she wasn't going to take care of herself, that left it to him to do it for her. They had one simple rule: He vetted all her dates. And sometimes, without her knowing, he'd scare them off. But that was really beside the point. It wasn't his fault she couldn't pick a decent guy.

He made a left turn on 10th Ave, right near the USB Theater, then he sped through Chelsea before making a left on 28th Street, heading toward Chelsea Piers. He made a right at the stop sign, turning onto her quiet street. The street was lined with lofts and new apartment high-rises, all boasting a name with Arms, or Manor.

Before she'd moved, Noah and his team researched the building's owners and the neighborhood crime rate. Everything to make sure she would be safe. Well as safe as she could be in Manhattan. It also didn't hurt that he watched her every move. And not in some creepy, stalkery way, but more like a big brother way. *Sort of…*

Never mind that. He drove past her building and around the back to the lot he paid for specifically for these kinds of situations. Yeah, so maybe he also paid most of her rent. She thought she'd gotten extremely lucky with a rent-controlled apartment in the heart of the city. In reality, he paid most of the tab. He also paid for two parking spots. Not that Lucia had a car. But in case she ever got one, she'd have somewhere safe to park it. Somewhere right next to the damn elevator. He paid almost as much to secure that spot as he paid for the apartment. His spot was in the darkened shadows somewhere she'd never think to look. He didn't mind though, because in most scenarios, he was the thing that went bump in the night.

"Matthias, talk to me. Where are they headed?"

"They're stopping for ice cream at Benny's then he's going to take her home."

Okay, so Noah had about ten minutes. Benny's was a local mom-and-pop ice-cream place about five blocks away. He jogged along the parking garage to the side stairs. While he'd insisted that she get a building with a doorman, there was no accounting for the additional exits and entrances into the building. Luckily, this one was exit only. Only confirmed residents had keys. Unfortunately, even your average guy could pick these locks, and he happened to be better than average.

In less than a minute, he was through the door and took the back stairway up to her apartment. She'd listened to him and employed the deadbolt. Problem for her was he had a key.

In seconds he turned off her security alarm. Well, at least there was that. Lucia had been so against it in the first place. At least she realized that a woman living alone needed *some* security. He glanced around and noted that she'd changed a few things. Was that a new pillow?

Matthias spoke into his earpiece. "You've got about five, boss. They've stopped outside the apartment. I'm going to go ahead and turn off the mic on her phone now if that's okay with you."

More judgment from the youngest member of the team. Whatever. He'd deal with that later. Now, the real question was where to wait for her.

What if she brought the guy in here?

Oh hell no. The mere idea of it had him gripping the edge of the countertop. She had better be coming in alone.

Didn't she know the first thing about dating? Damn it, this was their first date. She was supposed to make the guy twist in the wind for a bit first.

How many one-night stands have you had?

No. He was not going to think about that. It was different. That's all. Besides, Lucia was a good kid. And there was no way Nonna DeMarco would approve.

He'd give her a few minutes to run the guy off herself, and then the two of them were going to have another conversation about dating and personal safety.

She couldn't really be interested in this guy, right? He was boring. *Unlike you?* Noah grimaced. Yeah well, she didn't need to date anyone like him either. If she did, Noah would have to employ more drastic measures to keep her safe.

No. Lucia needed a nice guy, but someone more interesting than a records keeper.

Okay, if he was going to give her the chance to send Brent packing by herself, he needed to wait somewhere other than the living room. If she caught sight of Noah first, and if she was carrying that Taser he'd given her for Christmas, he might end up as fried toast. He jogged down the hallway and turned left into her bedroom, gently closing the door behind himself.

He hopped onto her bed, bouncing slightly and leaned back against the pillows. *I've always loved how girly she is*, he thought, enjoying the scent of her perfume in the room and looking around at the four-poster bed, the soft colors, and all the ruffled pillows. He also loved that when she completely lost her temper her curls went flying and her eyes snapped with anger.

It was probably why he enjoyed pissing her off so much.

Something caught his eye as he lay back against the pillows, readjusting them for his comfort. Her bottom drawer was open.

Do not open it. Leave it be. She won't appreciate — Oh fuck it.

He pulled it open and took out his phone, shining the flashlight directly inside.

"Well, well, well. What do we have here?"

This is a date. You should be having fun.

Lucia fixed her lipstick in the mirror at Benny's. She didn't need to use the bathroom. She was stalling. Stalling for time. Stalling for composure. Whatever. She wasn't sure what she was doing. Brent was really trying, but she was giving him a half-assed effort.

It wasn't like he wasn't interesting. He was. Yeah, okay, maybe he had no edge. But, there was more to life than edge, right? The guy skydived for the love of God. She should be totally into this. He ran triathlons, so that meant a great body. In theory, anyway.

Then why are you stalling? She swallowed hard.

She fluffed her curls, gently winding a couple of the loose strands around her finger to give them more bounce. Next, she fixed a nonexistent smudge of her lipstick.

Stop stalling. Go back to your date. He won't bite.

Maybe if he did you'd be more into this.

Stop it. Good Catholic girls don't want to be bitten.

No, but fun *Catholic girls do.*

What was wrong with her? He was cute. And God knew she needed a life. Hell, make that a sex life. It wasn't like she never had any other takers. She'd dated some. But no one who interested her in that deep primal way.

Except for Noah.

And go ahead and mark that under, *Never. Going. To. Happen*. Noah had been her brother's best friend. Noah fashioned himself responsible for her. Noah was also the biggest pain in the ass she'd ever met. He was always there, invading her life, her mind, her decisions — her family.

She couldn't throw a stone without running into him or one of the men who worked for him. Ever since Rafe had died, he'd made himself her surrogate big brother.

Problem was, as sexy as he was, most of the time she found it hard to look at him in a brotherly way.

Not going to happen so she needed to get that out of her head.

Besides, Brent was...great. He was the kind of guy she *should* want. He was the kind of guy she *should* be thinking about. Not some guy who was too sexy, too cocky, and too damn good-looking.

Everything about Noah Blake screamed, *Danger, Will Robinson, danger*. He was the kind of guy that she didn't know how to handle. The kind of guy who wanted a woman who knew what she was doing. And she was not that woman.

Forget about him. Focus on the guy who wants you. The guy sitting outside.

With a deep breath, she squared her shoulders. She could do this. She could play sexy vixen. For once, she didn't want to be the good girl. For once, she didn't want to be the one who was overlooked.

She wanted to feel sexy. She wanted to be *wanted*.

Lucia slid her gaze down to her purse and the manila envelope sticking out of the corner. *Are you sure you want him? Or do you just want what he can give you?* She shook her head. Yes, she'd agreed to go out with Brent, because well, he'd helped her. But he *was* good-looking. And interesting.

Who are you trying to convince?

Yes, she needed the information he'd gotten for

her. If it would help her track down who owned that house, and eventually her brother's murderer, then she was going to take it. Because that was all she'd ever wanted. Some answers about what happened to Rafe. She deserved those answers. More importantly, her grandmother deserved those answers.

Rafe had always looked out for her. And if something had ever happened to her, she'd known that he would tear the world apart looking for answers. And looking to make someone pay.

But for the first time in a long time, she'd come to understand that she couldn't make Rafe her whole life. He'd been gone for six years. It was time to move on. The envelope could wait. Right now, she had a date and an ice cream waiting. Besides, Rafe wouldn't begrudge her a life. He may not be so thrilled about the *kind* of life she wanted, but he'd want her to be happy. And maybe Brent could give that to her.

Not likely. He's not Noah.

Dammit. She had to get Noah Blake off the brain. Lately it had gotten worse. She'd started to imagine heated glances from him. Whenever she was at his office, and she caught him looking at her, she would swear she saw...longing in his eyes. But that couldn't be right. Maybe more of an intensity? What the hell did she know?

All she knew was every time she caught him looking at her like that, she thought about using one of those toys JJ got her as a gag gift. The ones in her bedside drawer that no one knew about. The same ones that she put in a shoebox under her bed every time the cleaning lady came by.

She still flushed at the thought of the ridiculous party favor she'd gotten at that bachelorette party the prior month. The thing was insane. No one on earth was that big. It just wasn't possible. Though it wasn't like she had anything to go on.

If you want something to go on, stop hiding in the bathroom and go on your date.

Checking her appearance one more time, she forced a smile on her face. She was going to do this. She was going to go out there and have a good time and let Brent take her home. And then she was going to let him kiss her good night.

And then, instead of overthinking this, she was going to see where it went.

More resolute, she pushed open the door and grinned when she saw Brent standing there with two strawberry ice cream cones. He handed her one, and when some melted on her finger, he took her hand and gently licked it off.

Oh god. She fought the immediate urge to snatch her hand back. *Relax.* He's trying to be cute. Not creepy.

"Come on, let's head back," she said. They'd opted to park his car and just walk back to her place.

As they walked and ate their ice cream, the balmy summer breeze lifting a few of her curls, he said "I'm glad you agreed to go out with me. Although you should know, I wasn't above begging."

Lucia took another lick of her ice cream. "You're sweet."

He shrugged. "Not that sweet. I've seen you walk by the Café on fourth before. You can imagine my surprise when you walked into my office. I had to take a shot and ask you out."

Lucia wasn't used to quite so many compliments. Oh sure, *at first* guys were interested, but then something almost always happened to make them cool off. Most of her dates never went past date one. She was starting to think she was really bad at this. JJ said she just needed to date a few more frogs. Though, it seemed to Lucia that she'd had more than her fair share of them.

In the five blocks it took to reach her apartment, Brent regaled her with stories of his last bungee jumping trip.

"Okay, if I agree to go bungee jumping, where do you suggest I jump first?"

His answer was instant. "Over the Zambezi River in Zimbabwe, hands down."

She laughed. "Wait, I have to go all the way to Zimbabwe for my very first jump?"

"There's nothing like it with Victoria Falls thundering behind you. It'll be awesome."

"Okay, maybe I'll book that trip. But maybe, just maybe, we could try something closer to home first. Maybe not as majestic, but still thrilling."

They reached her apartment just as she finished

the last bit of her cone. She shifted on her feet nervously. This was it. The moment she was waiting for. Do or die. Well okay, not do or die, but close.

Brent stepped closer. "Thank you for agreeing to go out with me. And just so you know, I'm going to kiss you in a second. But first, I want to ask you out again. Don't worry we'll take it slow on the thrill rides. But I do want to see you. So what do you say...go out with me again?"

No. "I'd like that."

Despite everything in her body telling her that this was not the guy, she was deliberately ignoring it. He was nice. She couldn't wait for perfect. Sometimes nice and good-looking would just have to do.

He leaned forward, shifting his hand to cup her cheek, and stroking it gently. When he dipped his head down, she had to force herself still. He gently brushed his lips over hers. His lips were firm but undemanding. As if he was waiting for her permission.

He pulled back with a smile. "I'd like to be a gentleman and walk you upstairs if that's okay?"

Upstairs? As in, inside her apartment? Her heart thundered but not from desire. More like pure unadulterated nerves.

She could do this, right? Just because she didn't feel anything when he kissed her, it didn't mean anything. Maybe she just needed more time to get into it. This was the kind of guy that most girls would be drooling over. What was wrong with her?

She took his hand and smiled up at him. "Come on up."

The elevator ride was tense. Or maybe it was just tense to her because she had no idea what was going to happen. More kissing probably. But she had no idea how to do any of what came next. All she had to go on were a few heavy make out sessions. Mostly high school though.

JJ kept telling her she needed to have a one-night stand to just drop the V card already. And that way, she'd be a lot less nervous about it. And maybe she was right. Brent seemed to actually like her, so he was far better than a one-night stand.

Except, you're totally not into this.

Okay, that was beside the point. When the elevator doors chimed, a shiver stole up her neck, making the fine hairs stand on end. With a wan smile, she led the way to her apartment, pausing at the door. There were those shivers again. Like an alarm. Like a warning. Maybe just nerves?

"This is me." Turning the key, she let herself in and went to turn off the alarm, but it was already off.

She frowned. Her brain mentally rewound the day's events. She could see herself arming it. Or had she? Was her brain just replacing a memory from yesterday for today?

She closed the door behind them. "Would you like a drink?"

Brent shook his head. "No. All I want is you."

This was the part where Lucia was supposed to feel the butterflies right? Every brush of his fingers was supposed to feel as if she had electricity coursing through it? This was the part where she moaned into his embrace, right?

Except none of that was happening. Not even when he pulled her close, pressing their bodies together.

This was ... *Nice*. Perfectly pleasant. Maybe even a little warm. Warm was good, right?

Head in the game DeMarco.

She started slowly, leading him back toward the bedroom. Maybe if she got him there she'd get more in the mood. She'd have all the nice-smelling girly things in there which hopefully would feel more romantic.

He easily followed her lead. He made a moaning sound deep in his throat, and she only wished she wanted to make such a sound. A tiny annoying voice spoke up from deep in the recesses of her mind.

Are you sure you want to do this? You want your first time to just be ... fine?

No. She wanted hot. She wanted sexy. She wanted to tingle. She wanted to feel like a supermodel who'd found her accompanying rock star. But not everybody got a rock star. Sometimes nice was good.

She opened the door to the bedroom, and he continued to kiss her. But the more his tongue slid into her mouth, licking inside, the more she wanted to turn her head. She drew back, angling her head away slightly. He took that to mean that she wanted him to kiss her neck. With a little groan, he slid his lips along her jaw, then the column of her throat. But she was having a hard time getting into the mood.

All she kept thinking about was if she was doing this right. And God, she wanted to get out of her shoes. They were pinching her toes. And those growling noises he was making were actually kind of funny. When had she left her blinds open? While she was at it, she really needed to get some damn groceries.

This is not what you're supposed to be thinking about. There was something wrong with her. He was a perfectly nice guy wanting to rock her world. And she was thinking about her damn blinds and groceries.

I bet you wouldn't feel this way with Noah.

And just like that, heat raced through her bloodstream and her breath caught. Just thinking about him was enough to make her skin tight and itchy. Those butterflies she'd been concerned about, there they were, fluttering rapidly inside, making something deep in her core pull tight.

Still, Lucia fought it. There was no way she was going to think about Noah at a time like this. But, maybe that wasn't the end of the world. It was just a fantasy. Her brain latched on to what her body was craving. And the image of him in her mind formed and solidified.

Suddenly, it wasn't Brent kissing her throat, it was Noah. But his lips weren't quite as soft. They were firm. Sure. Knew exactly what he wanted and exactly how to get the right response from her.

There was no thinking about anything else when she was with him. Only the sensation of being in his arms. The sensation of her heart hammering so fast it nearly beat out of her chest. The feeling she sometimes got when he looked at her and all her bones felt like jelly. That was how it was meant to be with Noah.

A little dangerous. Definitely bad for you. But oh so good.

Lucia slid her hands into Noah's hair, tugging a little. He muttered a soft curse against her throat, his hands holding her flush against him. Through his jeans she could feel the pulse of his erection against her center.

Yes. This was much more like it.

His kisses grew more frantic. His hands less patient. They skimmed over her hips with a strong grip. Before sliding his thumbs up over her belly and over her ribcage, just under her —

"Okay, Romeo. I think that's enough."

Lucia squeaked, then jumped away from Noah — err, Brent. *Right Brent*. Her date. Noah, the idiot, was on her bed.

"Wha–What the hell are you doing here, Noah?"

Noah lay back against her pillows. His feet were on her bed with his shoes on, she noticed with irritation. He looked comfortable. Completely relaxed, as if he belonged there. *Wouldn't you like that?*

"Well, it looks like I'm just in time to interrupt."

Brent stared between her and Noah, then back again. "I thought you said you didn't have a boyfriend."

Lucia turned her attention to him and placed a reassuring hand on his arm. "I don't. The intruder on my bed is my wannabe big brother. *And he was just leaving.*"

Noah shook his head. "No such luck, princess. You don't know this dude from a can of paint. We had a deal. You let me check out anyone you want to go out with. You seem to have forgotten that."

"We never had a deal. You just seem to think that you can dictate to me. You can't!"

Brent interjected. "I should probably be going."

Lucia gripped his forearm harder. "No. Stay. Noah is going. Aren't you Noah?"

Noah grinned, his devilish smile bringing a mischievous twinkle to his eyes. Looking at the two of them in close proximity, Lucia could see clearly that there was no competition. Noah had dark sooty lashes that framed those intense whiskey-colored eyes, high cheekbones, a straight Roman nose, and full lips that tilted crookedly when he smiled. The man was gorgeous and he knew it. Which was a problem, because he often used it to get what he wanted.

Brent, in comparison, also had dark hair, but not as dark as Noah's. It also didn't fall in disarray where some parts looked styled and other parts unkempt, but mostly looking like he'd just rolled out of bed. Or he'd rolled out of bed *with someone*. Brent's eyes were a pale blue. Kind. He was cute in that boy-next-door, all-American kind of way. He didn't look like he belonged in a fashion magazine, not like Noah did.

Feeling a little uncharitable for comparing Brent so unfavorably with Noah, she had to concede that he was at least tall. Not as tall as Noah, but few men could compare to Noah's towering height. Besides it wasn't about looks, or height, or charisma, anyway.

Annoyed with herself, Lucia closed her eyes, hoping maybe this was all a bad dream, but when she opened them again he was still there. With Noah in the room, it was hard to breathe. He dominated everyone and sucked up all the air, silently pulling her towards him with his gravitational force alone. It was like poor Brent wasn't even there.

"Now, Lucia, I know you'd like to think you're in charge right now. But you're not. You don't know this guy. And you invited him back to your place? I thought I taught you better than that."

Brent tried to make an escape again. "Lucia, why don't you deal with this guy? And we'll try this again later."

"No. You're not going anywhere."

Noah pushed himself to a seated position on the edge of the bed. "Oh yes he is. Because you and I need to discuss what the hell this is for." He held up the party gift from the bachelorette party.

Oh no. Oh no. Oh no.

In that moment, Lucia prayed to every saint her grandmother had ever forced her to pray to. Prayed to the Virgin Mary then to Jesus. Heck, for good measure she added Buddha in there too. Just in case. But nothing happened. The ground did not open and swallow her.

Instead, she stood with her hand on Brent's arm, staring at Noah as he held up the largest purple dildo she'd ever seen in her life.

Brent's mouth fell open but no sound came out. As mortified as she was, Lucia couldn't really blame him. The stupid thing was over a foot long, and thick. Really, really thick. Like thicker than a cucumber. She'd certainly never used the thing. It was a gag gift.

"How dare you go through my things!" she squeaked.

Noah shrugged. "I didn't go through your things. The drawer was open. The thing was practically sticking out of it. Making its escape."

Next to her, Brent shifted his gaze to her.

"That's not mine," she whispered. "I m-mean it is but I've never used it. It's a gag gift from a bachelorette party." She swung her gaze to Noah. "*Put that down.*"

"Not a chance. I mean, this thing is fascinating. I'm no stranger to toys myself. As far as I'm concerned, they can always enhance the situation. I'm not one of those guys that feel jealous or threatened. Matter of fact, I'm all for a little solo play. But this thing..." He held it up and shook it around. "Even I've never seen anything like it. And I've had a lot of practice."

He turned his attention to Brent. "No disrespect to you, but I don't think you can live up to this. It vibrates *and* rotates! Even I feel a little frightened by this thing."

Screw the ground opening up and swallowing her whole. Just shoot her now. That would end this quickly. Shoot her. Send her little behind to heaven. Because she was done. Noah was bending the dildo around as it wiggled in his hands. He pushed the button, and the damn thing rotated on its own, making a whirring sound. *Oh God.* Could this get any worse?

Brent fixed his gaze on her. "I'm going to go."

"No, please don't go."

She lunged and grabbed at the dildo, tugging when Noah refused to release it. The silicone material bent in ways Lucia was sure it wasn't designed to as they fought over it. This was easily one of the most undignified moments of her life, but she just couldn't take it anymore. Noah's smug face as he watched her struggling to get a better grip on the wiggling, gyrating piece of plastic only made it worse.

"Ugh, let go!"

In a fit of sudden anger, Lucia kicked him in the shin. And in his surprise, Noah let go of his end of the toy. The next few seconds would forever play in her mind in slow motion as she watched the toy fly end over end and hit Brent directly in the face.

"Ouch!"

Lucia covered her mouth in horror as the toy fell to his feet. The silence that followed was only broken by the sounds of the still-running toy, wiggling over the carpet.

Noah guffawed. "My bad. Did I get it in your mouth? Don't worry, it doesn't mean anything. What's a little dick in the mouth between friends, am I right?"

"I have to go."

"No, wait!"

But Brent didn't wait. All she could hear were his footsteps as they echoed on the hardwood floors, down the hall, into her living room, then kitchen, and then the front door opening and slamming shut behind him.

With a deep breath, Lucia whirled on Noah.

"I swear to God I will make you pay if it's the last thing I do. You are going to pay so hard. What the hell is wrong with you? *You are completely shameless!*"

He grinned as he stood and then knelt to grab the toy, pushing the button on the dildo again. "I'm looking forward to it. This is the best laugh I've had in months."

He moved towards her, his gait smooth and predatory. He paused about a foot away, and she could smell the scent of sandalwood. She fought the urge to inhale deeply.

When he leaned close, Lucia held her breath.

"Next time, *I* check out the guy. And pick somebody tougher. If he'd stood up to me, I would have respected him more."

Lucia couldn't help it. Frustration was taking

over as the blood boiled under her skin. And the urge to hit him overwhelmed her.

"I hate you."

He took a step, bringing them so close they were almost touching. When he leaned over her again, she nervously licked her lips as her belly flipped.

His voice was low and sultry as he whispered. "No. You don't."

Chapter Three

It shouldn't have hurt so much to hear her say those words. *I hate you.* Especially when he knew it was just a reaction to finding him in her room. But even knowing that, it cut through him with all the precision of a knife and he was left with the curious sensation of a widening in his chest.

"You could never hate me, Princess."

Lucia's eyes flashed and he would have laughed if

he wasn't afraid she might actually try to attack. There wasn't much she could do to him, but more than likely she'd harm *herself* in the attempt and he couldn't allow that. Despite what she thought, everything he ever did was to protect her. Especially keeping her away from guys like the one he'd found her sucking face with just now.

Disgust had him glancing down at the monstrously large dildo in his hand.

"Did you really think that guy was going to get the job done if you're used to this?"

Lucia screeched and whacked him right in the middle of the chest. "I told you it's not even mine! Not really. It was a gift."

"What the hell kind of friend gives you a dinosaur dildo as a gift?"

"None of your business."

She tried to grab it, stretching on her toes as he raised his arm overhead. The position put her off balance and he instinctively held out an arm to steady her when her legs gave out. Her breasts crushed against his chest, and the soft curves he'd tried so hard to ignore were suddenly front and center in his brain, along with the enticing summer scent of her hair. She placed a hand on his waist as she straightened, and Noah knew a solid sixty seconds of true fear as all his blood shot below his belt.

He could not throw wood around Lucia.

Stand down. Stand down.

He chanted the order, praying the relevant pieces of

anatomy would get the message in time.

Lucia took advantage of his distraction and jumped, managing to snatch the dildo from his hand while simultaneously fulfilling every late-night fantasy he'd ever had about her.

"And for god's sake put it down!" She threw the still-rotating dildo on the bed before turning back to him, murder in her eyes.

"Okay, okay. I was just playing around."

Lucia pointed to the door. "Outside. Now."

He backed up, allowing her to push him out of the room and into the hallway. The evidence of what he'd only been able to hear earlier was all around them. The sky-high stilettos she always wore kicked off by the front door. Her jacket was discarded in the middle of the floor, torn off in a fit of passion, perhaps? Noah ground his jaw at the reminder of that guy's hands all over her. He wasn't anywhere near good enough for her.

And you are?

He shook off the thought. No one was good enough for Lucia, especially not him, but it was the least he could do to help her weed out the obvious losers. It was what Rafe would have done.

Hell, Rafe probably would have thrown that guy over the balcony for pawing his sister that way. Seriously, it was their first date and that asshole had actually thought a rushed screw was appropriate? Lucia was the kind of woman who deserved flowers and chocolates and candlelight. Not some frantic fuck against the wall. Though shit, just the idea was fucking hot: Lucia, sweaty and panting, him behind her lifting her skirt—oh and what do you know, his erection was back in full force.

Noah was so caught up in his thoughts, he barely noticed where she was pushing him until she had the front door open and he was in the hallway.

"Give me back my key." She held out her hand, her lips pursed into the most adorable pout.

He knew she was really pissed but couldn't resist tormenting her a little bit.

"Do you really think I need a key to get in here?"

Her deep breath told him how close he was to getting smacked again. But then suddenly her face changed and she shook her head sadly.

"You just don't get it, Noah. This is my life and no one is going to stop me from living it. Not even you. I have to grow up sometime."

"I'm not trying to stop you from living. I'm just trying to keep you safe."

"Safe, I understand. But this…this is too much. You're out of control. I have the right to my privacy and having you show up in the middle of my bedroom is kind of a buzzkill to my sex life, you know? So maybe next time we'll go to his place."

The fuck there would be a next time. He'd kill the asshole first. *There you go with your killer instinct again.* "Lucia…Don't do anything crazy." The thought of her at some guy's place, possibly somewhere he couldn't get to her if things went wrong, made him feel like he was having a heart attack. He put a hand over his heart to make sure it wasn't actually going to jump out of his chest the way it felt.

"Crazy like showing up in someone else's bedroom holding a dildo? I don't think you should be giving me advice in this particular situation. Although, I suppose I should thank you for finding that for me. Since Brent and I were interrupted, I guess I'll need it tonight."

Before he could process her words, the door was coming at him. He took a step back mere seconds before it would have hit him in the face.

He stood there for a few more minutes, listening to the sounds of her moving around the apartment before he finally left. She was upset right now, but she'd come around. She always did. Although he couldn't deny that something about tonight felt different. Not only that she'd actually stood up to him and thrown him out, but what she'd said about using that sex toy later. She had to have been joking about that, right? There was no way Lucia was that kinky. And, oh so helpfully, his brain offered an image of her, on her bed, legs splayed, head thrown back in ecstasy as that dildo worked its magic. His dick throbbed.

Fuck. *I wish* his cock seemed to say.

As he was descending the stairs, he hit the first speed dial on his cell phone. Matthias answered immediately.

"Hey, did you kill the surveillance on Lucia's place yet?"

There was a moment of silence before Matthias

responded. "You mean did we just see you get your ass handed to you? Nope, no idea what you're talking about."

Noah cursed. He could hear the muffled laughter coming through the line which told him Matthias wasn't alone in the office. Great. This was what he got for hiring a bunch of anti-social loners just like himself. They didn't have anywhere else to be on a Friday night either.

There was no way Jonas was ever going to let him live this one down.

"Whatever. I'll be in the office in a few."

He hung up and shoved his phone back in his pocket. Once he reached the parking garage, he looked up to Lucia's window. He watched as her shadow moved around the apartment before the light in the front went dark. Over the years, he'd been so many things to her as she grew up. Surrogate big brother. Protector. A shoulder to cry on.

But he'd never felt like he was on the outside looking in to her life.

He'd spent years knowing this time was coming. That there would be a day when she'd meet someone, a man without screwed-up ethics and a boatload of secrets. Someone who could love her the way she deserved and give her the things she needed. All the things he couldn't do. Noah had thought he was ready for when that day approached, but he'd had no idea how fast the years would go by.

I have to grow up sometime, she'd said, with no idea

what those words meant to him.

Yeah, he thought, *but not yet*. He couldn't bear to lose her yet.

Lucia stood in the middle of her living room for a moment, trying to process what had just happened. She rubbed her temples. Maybe if she pretended it hadn't happened this would all go away. But the evidence was all around her: her jacket on the floor and her lucky shoes by the door, the ones she only wore when she had a date.

Her lucky stilettos hadn't been so lucky tonight.

She groaned before stooping to pick up the shoes. Things had definitely not gone the way she'd expected. Poor Brent. All he'd done was have the misfortune of asking her out. How was he to know she had a crazy, over-protective pseudo-stalker who'd show up and cock-block him before he even got to second base?

She winced, imagining what he must think of her now. She hadn't even wanted to go on the date at first so she couldn't consider it too much of a loss, but damn, it was still embarrassing. Well, at least she didn't have to figure out a way to let him down easy.

Noah had taken care of that for her, she thought bitterly.

She cleaned up the living room and cut out all the lights before heading back to her room. Her face flamed at the sight of the large purple dildo on the bed. It was still running, the lights on the base blinking furiously as it moved around on the comforter. Lucia picked it up, and after mashing a few random buttons, she finally managed to turn it off.

Just looking at it made her angry all over again.

The anger had nowhere to go and because it made her want to scream, she picked up her phone and hit the second speed dial. The fact that Noah had programmed himself in on the first speed dial annoyed her all over again.

JJ answered on the first ring. "Why are you calling me? You're supposed to be on a date."

Lucia sighed. "I *was* on a date. He's gone now."

"Already? Please tell me you got laid at least?"

"I was close. Then Noah showed up."

JJ was silent for a moment. Then she exploded in laughter. "You have got to be fucking *kidding* me? Noah showed up in the middle of your date? Wait, go back and tell me everything."

Lucia settled herself on top of her comforter as she relayed the story. By the time she got to Noah showing up in her room and the dildo hitting Brent, JJ was laughing so hard she sounded like she was wheezing. As much as Lucia wanted to stay mad, she couldn't after retelling the story. It truly was the most ridiculous thing ever.

"So, he got nailed in the face, no pun intended."

There was a pause as JJ tried to rein in her laughter. "Then he just ran out?"

Lucia felt a sudden burst of shame on Brent's behalf. He really had just ditched her without looking back. Although considering how menacing Noah could appear at times, she couldn't really blame him. That was a battle he couldn't possibly win.

"What else could he do? Noah was in my room, *on my bed*, like a jealous ex-boyfriend. You know how he gets."

"Yes, I do. And so do you. Which makes me wonder why you don't just bone the guy already and put us all out of our virtual blue balls."

Her friend's words brought a rush of conflicting emotions. The usual denial mixed with an uncharacteristic blast of heat at the thought of getting naked with Noah. She wasn't sure when her thoughts about him began to change. One day he'd been good old Noah, the surrogate big brother who annoyed her one minute and delighted her the next.

Then one day she'd looked at him and everything was different. He was suddenly the smartest, most handsome, most masculine presence she'd ever been exposed to, and everything inside of her had taken notice all at once. It had made her feel both awakened and exposed to discover that she could feel these things for someone who had been a part of her life for so long.

"It's not like that between us. You know that."

JJ made a rude sound. "So you keep saying, but I have eyes. And that man is insanely sexy. There is no way you can be exposed to that kind of grade-A testosterone all the time and not feel anything. I don't believe it."

"Well, believe it. He's like another brother."

"I guess."

JJ didn't sound convinced, which only increased Lucia's agitation. Noah had never looked at her as anything other than the annoying young girl that he had to look out for. She was an obligation, a tie to a former life that he'd probably rather forget. As soon as she had the thought, she was ashamed. Noah had idolized her brother Rafe, and she didn't really think he wanted to forget about him. It would just be nice not to feel like an old debt that he was paying off.

"He only does this because he feels like it's what Rafe would do if he were here. But this time he's gone too far. He can't just break into my apartment whenever he wants."

"Well, it sounds like it's time for a little payback."

JJ was known for her creative and diabolical thinking so if she had a plan, Lucia was all in. It would be nice to feel like she had the upper hand with Noah for once. Maybe even give him a little taste of what it was like to have someone butting into your life at the most inopportune moment.

"What do you mean by payback?"

JJ chuckled in a way that told Lucia she already had an idea. "I have just the thing."

Immediately, Lucia had second thoughts. Did she really want to start a war with Noah? Not that she ever thought for even a moment that he would hurt her, but JJ had a tendency to be a little…inappropriate. Following her advice for payback would be like adding gasoline to a fire that was already dangerously close to raging out of control.

Then she got a mental image of Noah holding that stupid dildo and waving it around. She wrinkled her nose. No, he'd brought this all on himself.

"What do you have in mind?"

JJ chuckled. "Do you have anything against public nudity?"

Later that night, Lucia was snuggled under the covers when she finally remembered the envelope. It was hard to believe, but in all the hustle and excitement of having a date and then the showdown with Noah, she'd completely forgotten about it.

Throwing the comforter back, she swung her legs over the edge of the mattress and stood. Her handbag was still out front where she'd left it on the couch. She walked slowly, navigating the apartment in the dark. Her fingers fumbled over the lamp on the side table until she was able to turn the switch, and the room filled with light. Her bag was still right where she'd left it. It was kind of amusing that it was still in the same spot after the wild events of the evening.

The thought brought back everything that had happened with Noah. *What the hell was wrong with him lately?* He'd always been over the top, but this was somehow different. She ignored the nagging sense that it was different because *she* was different. The same things that wouldn't have bothered her in the past were suddenly excruciating in light of the annoying, completely inappropriate feelings she'd been having whenever he was around.

Just let it go already, Lucia.

She slung her handbag over her arm and then turned the light off before retracing her steps back to her room. The envelope had gotten slightly smashed under her wallet and keys so she gently smoothed it with her fingers before taking it back to bed with her. Under the covers, she hesitated before pulling up the flap. Now that the moment was here, part of her wondered if it wasn't better to leave the past in the past.

When she'd first started searching for more details about her brother's murder, she'd still been completely mired in grief. Her mind had been focused solely on getting answers and filling in the gaps that her own memory refused to fill. Now that so much time had passed, she'd finally settled in to a life of her own and things were good. Did she really want to know what had happened that day? What if she couldn't handle it? It wasn't as if knowing who was responsible would bring her brother back.

But it would give her some closure, wouldn't it? At

least she'd know why. Even if it wouldn't bring Rafe back, it would mean something to her to know the people responsible for her brother's death had been brought to justice. She wasn't as much of an idiot as her brother and Noah had assumed. She was aware that he hadn't always lived his life on the straight and narrow. But no matter what he'd done, he didn't deserve to die the way he had. No one deserved that.

Wiping away the tears that had spilled over on her cheek, Lucia lifted the flap of the envelope and pulled out the piece of paper inside. It was a copy of a deed of sale.

HoloCorp, Inc.

Her heartbeat stuttered for a moment and then hammered against her ribcage. It was just a name, but it was more than she'd ever had before. And this time she had exactly what she needed to follow the breadcrumbs.

More like exactly *who* she needed, she thought as she grabbed her cell phone and scrolled through her contacts list. When she found the name she was looking for, she tapped the screen before she could change her mind.

"Lucia? Is everything okay?"

She smiled. Matthias always sounded worried when she spoke to him, something she found endearing. It was interesting that the same words from Noah made her feel smothered, but they just seemed sweet when coming from Matthias. Then again, he was a gentle sort of guy, always more worried about what she needed than himself.

The fact that he had a bit of a crush on her was part of it, too. And in all honesty, he was a much better choice for her. He was cute. It was kind of ridiculous actually. Like Noah put "No Uglies" on the job description. And Matthias was sweet. No way would he ever invade her privacy. Then why *not* Matthias? The answer was simple. He wasn't Noah. He was missing that raw sexual edge.

"I'm fine. How are you?" The sounds in the background got abruptly louder and Lucia giggled when she heard what sounded like sighs and feminine moans. "Are you guys watching porn over there?"

There was a beat of silence. "No! Uh, that was just Jonas being an asshole." After a brief pause, all the sounds receded. "Sorry about that. Uh, what's up?"

"I need a favor."

"Of course. Anything for you."

"Um, a favor you can't tell Noah about."

He was quiet, and Lucia felt even worse. She was asking him to choose her over his friend and boss. It normally wasn't something she'd ever do. His crush on her was an open secret amongst their group, and she had always made an effort to be considerate of his feelings. Lucia wasn't the kind of girl who considered a man's feelings a weapon to use against him. But in this particular case, it was a risk she'd have to take in light of what she was asking him to do.

"I normally would never ask you to do that but…I wasn't sure who else to call."

Matthias sighed. "You can always call me. You know that. What do you need?"

"To track down the owners of a corporation. All I

have is a deed to a property purchased in the corporation's name. That's probably not enough, but it's all I've got."

"It's no problem. Send me what you have and I'll see what I can do."

Suddenly, she heard Jonas's voice in the background. "Why are you hiding out in here? Are you sexting?"

"No, I'm not sexting. It's Lucia."

"Why are you sexting with Lucia? I'm telling…"

"*No one is sexting*," Matthias shouted, sounding exasperated.

"Hi, Lucia!" Jonas yelled.

Matthias groaned. "Dude, stop yelling in my ear."

"I'm just trying to say hi."

"She heard you. I'm pretty sure everyone in the building heard you."

Lucia covered her mouth to keep from laughing. All the guys on Noah's team were like family at this point. Family that fought and bickered constantly, but would walk through fire to protect their own.

"Tell him I said hello."

"She says hello. Now go away." Matthias relayed the message in a grumpy voice.

"Okay. Well, I know you guys are busy so I'll go now. Thanks for your help, Matthias. And remember, don't tell–"

"Yeah, yeah. Don't tell Noah. Got it."

Right before she hung up, she heard Jonas's voice again. "Don't tell Noah? Good luck with that. He's for sure going to find out about your sexting."

As Lucia turned out the light, she could only hope they wouldn't need luck.

Chapter Four

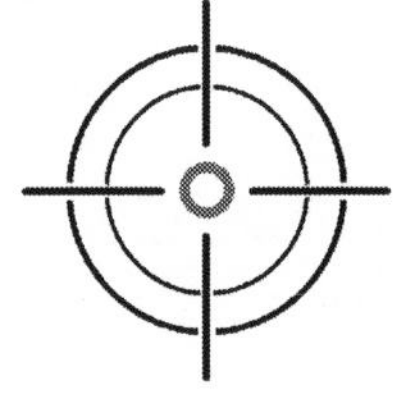

Noah checked his phone to see if there were any messages from Lucia. Nothing. It had been a few days since he'd seen her and she was still pissed off at him. Whatever. It was for her safety.

Are you sure about that?

Noah shoved away the thought and dragged his

attention back to his workout. Angrily he pushed the button to increase his speed on the treadmill. Outside the window, he watched the throng of passersby and tourists on the streets down below in Midtown as police attempted to direct traffic.

Man, did he love this city.

As a thief on the streets below, he'd never thought he'd end up here now. It was a long way from where he'd started to here. And he didn't take any of it for granted.

Bouncing around from foster home to foster home, he got to see a lot of the city. Unfortunately, he spent most of that time picking the best marks. And nowhere was better for marks than Midtown. Times Square.

But now…now instead of looking at them as targets, he saw them as the people he protected. *Sometimes.* Other times he was the bad guy.

But that's not who you are anymore. That's not what you do.

Back then, when he'd saved Ian's life, he hadn't considered where that one action would lead. The dark and twisty path it would take him on. That path had exploited his best skills and nurtured his darkest ones. Despite that, he considered himself lucky. He'd helped people. Saved them. But saving those lives came at a cost.

And when the cost got too high, he'd gotten out.

Noah pushed himself on the treadmill, running until his lungs burned and his eyes watered. Until his heart thundered against his ribs, begging for mercy. When he finally hit the stop button and the treadmill slowed, he dragged in deep breaths, completely unaware that he wasn't alone.

Then he turned and startled when he saw Jonas leaning against the glass doors of the gym.

"You're going pretty hard there," the other man commented as he pushed off the doors and walked closer.

"*Jesus Christ*, Jonas. You're a silent motherfucker, you know that? I may consider putting a bell on you."

Jonas just shrugged his big shoulders. "You're welcome to try."

Noah grabbed a towel and wiped his face. "You want to tell me why you're standing there staring at me like you got a crush? Or do you want me to guess?"

Jonas chuckled and shook his head. And he still didn't say anything. Jonas knew him better than anyone. He was his oldest friend.

"What's up, Jonas? You're creeping me out."

"Well, I was sort of hoping you could tell me. You've been out of it the last week. Lucia still not returning your calls?"

Noah knew a loaded question when he heard it. For years, Jonas had pestered him about Lucia. Jonas was the only one who knew how Noah felt about her.

"No, I haven't heard from her. She'll settle down. See it my way eventually."

"You sure about that? Either date her yourself, or cut her loose to do what she wants to do."

Noah shook his head. "You know I can't do that.

I'm supposed to be looking out for her. So if she can't choose wisely, then I'm going to make a nuisance of myself until she learns."

Jonas rolled his eyes. "How's that plan working out for you?"

Like shit. But there was no way Noah was telling his friend that. "It's working fine. Get the team ready. I'll need five for a shower."

After his shower, he joined his assembled team in the conference room. Matthias, with his two laptops and earpiece in his ear. Jonas at the other head of the table lounging back in the chair, his feet kicked up, gleaming loafers on display.

Oskar sat in front of his laptop looking irritated. But then, that was Oskar. The German rarely smiled. That was probably a good thing given the number of female clients who openly stared at him in interest. If he started smiling back at them, it might be pandemonium.

Ryan and Dylan rounded out the group. They were the newest additions. So far they'd proven themselves on assignments, but he was still testing them out.

"Okay guys." He shook out his hair, wiping away the last remnants of water. "So we had a few new clients come in. And a few repeat requests. Alana Brooks, the singer, is coming back to town and has an open spot for bodyguard duty. Ryan, you worked with her before. You willing to do it again?"

"Yeah, that's fine. Though if she insists on going to a

mall again, I'm getting back up. Those teenyboppers are scary people."

Everyone laughed. Even Oskar.

"You're afraid of a couple of teenagers?" Dylan asked.

"Laugh all you want but those girls can be dangerous. One jumped on my back in an attempt to climb over me and get to her." He shuddered. "That shit was terrifying."

Matthias laughed. "The great Ryan Delaney taken down by a couple of teenage girls."

Noah knew the kid had a point. There was nothing more frightening in their world than an unknown variable. A screaming girl determined to get to the object of her affection definitely qualified because you could never predict how far they'd go to get what they wanted.

"Okay, I'll put you down. We've also got the Boynton Corporation. They want us to take a look at their security setup. They've had a couple of internal break-ins."

Jonas nodded. "I can do the initial intake if you want."

Noah nodded. With their current caseload, he'd been relying on Jonas more and more. Maybe it was time to give his friend a raise.

They reviewed a few additional new cases. One for the FBI, who wanted to borrow Matthias's skills. For that one, Noah would do initial intake himself. He didn't trust the Feds.

After going through the rest of their new cases, he

brought up the last item on the agenda. "So, we've got a few pro bono cases on the docket."

Oskar groaned. "How are we ever supposed to make money if you keep taking pro bono cases?" Taking jobs that didn't bring in money made the German twitchy.

But he hated scumbag abusers more than any of them. Which was why, even though he grumbled, he was usually first in line for ass-kicking duty.

Besides, Noah had used his buy-out from ORUS to start this place. He'd put that money to good use. Oskar had helped him invest wisely, and those returns went to running Blake Security. That didn't mean Oskar wasn't wired to obsess over the bottom line.

"For every three jobs we take a pro bono one. That's how it works. You want to let this latest scumbag roam free?" What Noah didn't say was that he felt like he needed to do the penance.

Oskar harrumphed. Crossed his arms and sat back. "Whatever."

Noah fought his grin. That was his friend's way of saying 'Fine. Who do we have to save now?'

Noah nodded at Matthias, who put up the picture of their new client, a smiling young girl with a long brown ponytail.

"This is Ella Wielding."

Matthias popped up another picture, this time a man in his forties. Dark, greasy hair, scraggly beard, beady little eyes.

"This is her neighbor, James Thorne. He's been following Ella. Ella's mother has gone to the police about his inappropriate interactions with her daughter. Ella insists that she's seen him at the mall, when she's at soccer practice, and out with her friends. So far he hasn't touched, but that's just a matter of time. I want everything we've got on this guy."

Oskar sat forward, his brow furrowed deep. "What's our endgame?"

Everyone knew what he was asking. Oskar wanted to know if they were going to hand out police justice or street justice. One of those would land James Thorne in the East River.

Noah didn't flinch. "It depends on what we find. If he's done this before, repeatedly, I'd like to permanently *rehome* him somewhere he'll never hurt anyone again."

Oskar nodded his approval, but Jonas pinned Noah with a level gaze. Ryan and Dylan looked unperturbed. Matthias didn't even look up from his computer. They were all okay with it if guys like this no longer walked the planet.

While Oskar could be downright savage if it meant saving an innocent, Jonas believed in truth, justice and the American way. But even his friend had seen way too much injustice of late. Jonas knew who Noah was. What he'd done before he opened Blake Security.

The guilt that Noah carried around.

Jonas acted as his conscience. And when it couldn't be helped, Noah actually listened to his conscience. But if James Thorne turned out to be the lowest of the low, then

Noah might let his old self out to play.

Because sometimes you just had to take out the trash.

"Matthias, find us anything you can. Then we'll decide what to do with James Thorne."

Lucia eyed herself in the full-length mirror attached to her closet door. Mentally she ran through the checklist of things Nonna was sure to scrutinize and chastise her for.

Skirt length, check.

Blouse tucked in, check.

Hair smoothed back into a simple clip, check.

Earrings in, check.

She sighed. Because God forbid she didn't have earrings on when she went to see her Nonna. She loved her grandmother. She really did. But the woman had antiquated ideas about how a woman was supposed to present herself at all times.

Once Lucia had made the mistake of not wearing proper undergarments to bed as a teenager, and she'd thought her grandmother would faint from distress when she'd woken her for school the next morning.

Lucia had asked her what the big deal was about not wearing underwear to bed. Plenty of her friends did it and claimed it was more comfortable. What was the worst that could happen? All her Nonna had been able to get out between pinched lips was that it was improper. And what would happen if there were some emergency and they had to evacuate their building in the middle of the night?

Lucia hadn't had the nerve to point out that in the event of an emergency, she doubted anyone would care if she was bare-assed beneath her nightgown.

Growing up, Nonna had also had specific requirements about how a young lady should dress. Particularly, skirt length. Nothing above the knees, as it was vulgar. Blouses should always be tucked in to minimize sloppiness. Plus they must also not be too tight, in order to minimize generous curves.

She looked down at her boobs. Yeah, no minimizing those. And the hair. Well, Nonna had never been particularly happy with Lucia's curls. They'd spent hours upon hours trying to smooth out every last hint of curl.

As Lucia had gotten older, she'd let some of those things go. Besides, she looked better with waves anyway. Although, she secretly loved her wild curls. Besides, really, who had time for blow-drying? Especially not with her job.

The job was another point of contention. Nonna did not approve of fashion as a profession. Or even as a hobby. Which meant Lucia had been forced to sneak in her *Vogue* and *Vanity Fair* magazines. She'd hidden them under her mattress like she supposed some guys would hide dirty magazines. She'd been far less concerned about the salacious romance novels JJ had asked her to hide, since Nonna devoured them, too.

Lucia figured she couldn't complain too much. JJ's mom had been a renowned snooper. There was no getting anything past her. Nonna, while occasionally self-righteous, didn't look very hard. Under the mattress was a decent hiding place in her house. Lucky for Rafe. She smiled thinking of her brother. He'd always been a handful but he'd been so much fun. The best big brother a girl could have.

Outside of the aging brownstone in Queens where she'd grown up, Lucia tugged open the creaking glass door before turning the brass knob of the main door. Damn, it was unlocked. Her grandmother really needed to tighten up the security around here.

Awesome. Now she sounded like Noah. And that was the last thing on earth she wanted. That meddling self-righteous asshole.

With a deep breath, she stepped into the house and was instantly greeted by the scent of garlic and tomatoes. It smelled like home. She missed being here. She missed knowing that no matter what, Nonna was always going to be cooking and fussing about how she didn't eat enough. And at the same time fussing about her figure.

She found her grandmother in the living room dusting.

"Nonna, what are you doing? You're supposed to be recovering from pneumonia. Besides, I got you a cleaning lady so that you wouldn't have to do all this bending and reaching to clean."

Nonna wrinkled her nose. "You know I don't like someone poking around my house."

"Well, I know for a fact that she comes every week because I've been paying her. What does she do if you don't let her clean?"

A slight flush tinted her grandmother's cheeks. "Okay, so sometimes I feed her. The poor thing is so skinny. How is she going to get a good husband if she doesn't eat?"

Lucia could only sigh. Okay, new rules and a new cleaning lady, this one older. Someone Nonna couldn't push around so easily.

"I do these things so that you can be taken care of even when I'm not here. You have to let me help."

"Nonsense. I can take care of myself."

Lucia crossed her arms. "Do I need to remind you that you've been very ill? You should be resting. Let someone else take care of you for once."

Nonna waved her off. "I'm a grown woman. I'll tell you —"

A knock at the door stopped the argument mid-flow.

"Are you expecting anyone?"

She held up a hand to prevent Nonna from going to open the door. Nonna shook her head in amusement.

"Yes, actually, I am expecting someone. I have a life, too, young lady."

Lucia laughed. What was wrong with her? She'd

become nearly as paranoid as Noah. After peering through the peephole, she opened the door to find a dark-haired man on her grandmother's steps.

"Can I help you?"

He smiled broadly showing straight, blindingly white teeth. "I'm here to see Rosa DeMarco. I'm a doctor."

He didn't look like her Nonna's doctor. She glanced back at her grandmother. "Nonna?"

Her grandmother grinned, pushing her aside to open the door and welcome him.

"Antonio! I'm so glad you were able to come by to check on me."

Nonna stepped back to let him by and he walked straight into the living room as if he knew his way around. Lucia had no choice but to follow them both. Her grandmother sat on the couch watching with avid interest as he pulled out a stethoscope and blood pressure pump.

Lucia watched the two of them with mounting suspicion. "So, how long have you been my grandmother's doctor? And do you work with Dr. Erlichman?"

Dr. Antonio opened his mouth to answer, but Nonna answered for him.

"You remember my friend Esther? Well, this is her grandson, Antonio. Obviously, he's a doctor. And while he's home helping her out for a month, he checked on me. Especially since I was ill. He wanted to make sure that I was following all my doctor's orders."

Antonio nodded. "It's no trouble. My grandmother

lives three doors down. So after I check on her, I look in on your grandmother." He flashed another grin.

Lucia licked her lips. Something was up. She could feel it. "Well, I am grateful. Nonna doesn't usually let anyone help her. She's very independent."

He chuckled. "Oh, I'm well acquainted with her. That's why I was so surprised she asked me to check up on her every now and again. I'm sorry I was late today. I got held up with a friend in Brooklyn."

Lucia cocked her head. "Oh, did you guys have a set appointment? I would've taken my time getting here if I'd known that."

Lucia got the distinct impression her grandmother wanted her to arrive just when she had. Just in time to meet Dr. Antonio. Who, for all intents and purposes, was very good-looking. Tall, lean, thick dark hair. Everything about him screamed, 'I'm a good Italian boy.' But Lucia was in no mood.

"Okay then, I'll leave you to it. I have phone calls to make anyway."

The old lady thought she was tricky. Damn, she'd had to run out of her office, change in the building bathroom, hop two trains and a bus just to get here at the specific time her grandmother said she needed her. Under normal circumstances, she would have come on Saturday. But her grandmother said she'd been feeling weak since her illness, so of course Lucia had wanted to check on her.

You've been played.

Thirty minutes later, after Dr. Antonio came into

the kitchen to say goodbye to her, Lucia faced off against her grandmother.

"You think I can't recognize a set up when I see one?"

Nonna rolled her eyes. "Lucia, all I'm trying to do is introduce you to some nice Italian boys. Who knows the kind of people you're meeting in the city? Antonio goes to church. He's a doctor. You could do worse. Honestly, you act like I'm trying to force you into an arranged marriage. All I'm doing is introducing you. He thinks you're very pretty."

Lucia threw her hands up. "Nonna, that is not the point. I'm sure he is a very nice guy." But not Noah. She shoved that thought far aside. "I'm just not looking to date anyone right now."

Her grandmother scoffed. "Instead, what? You're running around playing sleuth? Trying to find out what happened to your brother? That's not the kind of life I want for you. I want you to be married and have babies, not skulking around in the dark looking in places you shouldn't be."

It was an old argument. Lucia turned to the stove and turned on the kettle. "I appreciate what you're trying to do. And I know you just want me to be happy. But you can't rule my life. Between you and Noah, I could use some breathing room."

Lucia reached for the tea but the box on the counter was empty. She spotted a large tin behind the flour. Maybe

Nonna had started putting her teas in there. She pulled out the can to open it. But instead of tea, there was a wad of cash.

Holy hell.

"Nonna. What is this?"

Her grandmother snatched the container out of her hand with more force than Lucia had ever seen her use. "It's just something I keep for a rainy day."

"That must be some rainy day you're expecting. Is there a tsunami coming? That's a lot of money, Nonna. There must be thousands of dollars in there."

Nonna closed the lid quickly and shoved it back behind the other canisters. "Yes. I've been saving for years. A little bit here, a little bit there. I find ways to save money. That's money I use just in case." She squared her shoulders. "I'm an old lady. I'm entitled to some secrets."

Lucia chuckled. "As long as those secrets don't include more men for me to meet, that is fine."

But even as she made her cup of tea and one for her grandmother, Lucia wondered what other secrets her Nonna was hiding.

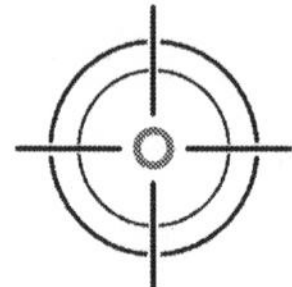

Lucia's feet were killing her. By the time she got home, the penny loafers had pinched so much she was convinced she'd never walk right again. Nonna didn't approve of stilettos and high heels. Which was a real bummer because they were pretty and, well, her boss insisted that she wear them.

The shoes her grandmother would prefer she wear were uncomfortable as hell. Once she got home, the first thing she did was kick them off inside her door. She tossed the mail onto the counter and then limped over to the couch and plopped down. She quickly checked her emails on her phone.

She grinned when she saw the confirmation for the surprise she'd set up for Noah. He would be livid. But he was the one who'd started their little war, so turnabout was fair play. And this was perfect. Because she would also get back at the gang at Blake Security for that little prank they'd pulled on her last Halloween.

Whoever thought up acting out *The Shining* in a warehouse building was seriously sick. She blamed Matthias. He might look sweet, but he was secretly devious.

If this surprise didn't get Noah off her back she didn't know what would. She relaxed against the cushions of the couch, allowing the tempting pull of sleep to close in around her, but then she turned her head.

No. She needed food first. And food was all the way over there—in the fridge.

Food was overrated, right? The more she gave any credence to the thought the more her stomach rumbled. "Okay, fine. I'll get up."

She pushed herself to standing and winced with

every step as she padded into the kitchen. She pulled together the makings of a quick soup and preheated the oven for some bread Nonna had sent home with her. It wasn't much, and it definitely wasn't fancy, but for now it would do. This week she'd been so busy she'd been flying by the seat of her pants as far as meals went.

She stared at the pile of mail and sighed. Eventually, she started sorting through the stack. Mostly bills. A few magazine subscriptions. That had been her major indulgence when she moved out on her own, openly getting a magazine subscription to every major fashion magazine. Eventually it had started to add up so she'd pulled back to just a few, but they were still her guilty pleasure. She was lucky she'd found a rent-controlled apartment so she could afford the little splurges like this.

She methodically went through the bills, putting most of them away to deal with later while making a mental note to call the student loan office. Then she was down to one last envelope. Plain manila. Her address typed.

No return address.

She frowned. No postmark. Could it have come from the Housing Association? They occasionally would drop leaflets or notices into everyone's mailbox. Most of those were mailed, but it was possible that they'd decided to hand-deliver something. It must be pretty urgent. She flipped over the letter and there were no markings or logos on the back. Just a plain envelope. Putting a finger under a small gap, she peeled it open and pulled out the letter inside. As she unfolded it, she noted there was only one line of text:

Stop. Digging.

A cold chill ran up her spine as the letter floated to the counter.

Oh shit. Did someone know what she was up to? How was that even possible? Who would care? She'd been careful and wasn't advertising what she was doing. Why would her getting answers now be a problem for anyone? Did that mean she was finally on the right track?

She'd gone with her brother that day as he was in a panic to stop something from happening. But what? For the past two years, she'd become obsessed with remembering. She'd written down everything she could remember but not a single memory cast any light onto that day.

She'd even tried hypnosis once. That had backfired. While she'd been very relaxed at first, she'd burst into tears as she'd tried to force her mind back to that memory.

That day in her life was like a big black hole.

At least she had the first memory of the day with Rafe on Coney Island. Anything after he got that phone call was a complete blank until the next morning when she woke up expecting to see her brother, but instead was told by Nonna that he was gone.

She'd been looking for answers ever since. She *needed* those answers. Because if she didn't have them, how would she ever mend the hole in her heart? *Keep pushing and you won't have a heart anymore,* she thought as she looked down at the message. Were the answers she needed worth dying for?

She picked up the letter. Maybe not. Maybe she did need to let go. Maybe for once she needed to listen to Noah and her Nonna and just get on with life. Walk away. Pretend that she could be normal. Is that what Rafe would want for her? Could she do that though? Could she just walk away and let it go? Her eyes glanced back at the sheet of paper. What if this time, it didn't just affect her? What if it affected Nonna, too?

She didn't need any more persuading. She ran back to the couch, picked up the phone and typed out a quick message to Matthias.

- That thing I asked you for? Never mind. Just leave it alone. I don't need to know anymore.

She tossed her phone on the couch and scrubbed her hands over her face. Maybe this was for the best. Rafe would want more for her than a life of looking over her shoulder.

Chapter Five

Lucia still wasn't talking to him.

Most days when he woke up, he wasn't thinking about anything in particular. He'd always been a light sleeper, useful when you never know if you'll wake with a gun to your head. But even once Rafe had taken him in, he'd always started each day as a blank slate. He wasn't happy or sad, just resigned to do whatever was necessary to make sure he survived to see the next morning.

But that day he'd woken with a cloud of foreboding. It was a strange thing to feel so much when you weren't used to giving a shit about anything. He hadn't really understood how familiar he'd become with Lucia's gentle intrusion in his life. Her soft glances and constant questions had started out as annoying and then became reassuring. Somehow he'd grown accustomed to someone caring about him.

But for the last week he'd had an abrupt return to what life was like before. No Lucia stopping by the office to bring him a home cooked meal. No calls to ask if he'd come by and fix something or kill a bug. No hugs that made him feel like a heart still beat somewhere within him. She was angry with him, and although she'd been mad at him before, this was different.

Maybe this is the new normal, he thought as he walked down a level to the office over two hours later than his usual time. He'd overslept for the first time in years and it only added to his cranky mood.

Noah's first clue that it wasn't going to be a typical day was seeing that Matthias was waiting for him in the common area.

"Yes, he just got here." Matthias hung up then, looking exasperated. "Did you forget we had a new client intake this morning? I tried calling your phone."

Damn. He never fucked up with clients. "Sorry, I overslept."

By the twitch in his eyebrow it was clear Matthias wanted to call bullshit on that, but wisely he didn't say anything. Noah walked past him and into the conference room.

"My apologies, we can start now. I'm Noah Blake and I hope the others have already introduced themselves."

The men sitting around the table nodded and smiled. They all looked extremely young and more likely to be on their way to a frat party than a business meeting. He looked down at the new client form that Matthias placed in front of him. Their firm was listed as owning and operating a chain of fitness centers. Suddenly, the fact that they all had those awful orange spray tans and more muscles than your average desk jockey made sense. This should be a pretty easy intake all around. Which was a good thing, since he was exhausted and definitely not functioning at full tilt.

"So, tell me what brings you to Blake Security gentlemen."

"Actually, we came by to deliver a message," said one of the men sitting directly across from Noah. "Jason, hit the music!"

All three of the men stood suddenly and ripped their shirts open, revealing oiled-up chests and six-pack abs. Rock music blared from somewhere that Noah couldn't identify.

What. The. Fuck.

Two seconds went by in complete, stunned silence before there was an explosion of movement and multiple weapons aimed in every direction. Next to him, Jonas had his Glock 9 pointing at the new client directly across from him, and Noah had his Sig Sauer aimed at the man across from him. Oskar had the guy who'd been sitting next to him in a headlock. The guy's face was bright red and going nearly purple.

The man across from Noah held his hands up slowly. "Well, this isn't the usual response to a birthday-gram."

"Wait, what?" Noah asked through clenched teeth.

He held up the card in his hand and wiggled it. Noah indicated with his head for Matthias to go get it. Matthias took the card gingerly and opened it. Suddenly he snorted. He walked over to Noah and held out the neon green card.

"It's just a birthday card."

"I thought they said they had a message for us?"

"We do," one of the guys interjected. "A message from Lucia. Can we put our hands down?"

"Yes." Noah nodded at the others to let the men go.

As soon as all their weapons were sheathed, the men glanced at each other and then one by one they ripped off their slacks, the tearing sound of fabric startling Noah so much he almost drew his gun again.

"Happy Birthday, Noah!" They screeched in unison and then proceeded to sing. Every time they sang "Happy Birthday," they shimmied and gyrated in unison until their extremely tiny banana hammocks were dangerously close to giving up the fight.

Oh. Fuck. No.

Just what he needed on top of a night of no sleep; a

room full of dudes with their dicks hanging out.

He opened the card and immediately recognized Lucia's handwriting. Just the sight of it brought a jolt of unexpected warmth to his heart. Until the three men approached, gyrating and rolling their abs as they finished the song, flinging their arms up at the end. In the silence that followed, the only sound was their breathing and Oskar's muffled laughter behind him.

Jonas clapped and Matthias joined in.

"Thank you. This has definitely made things more interesting around here, and it's not even my birthday," Jonas boomed.

"Or mine," Noah added under his breath, coughing when Jonas elbowed him in the gut.

"Yes, thank you." He bit out the words, figuring if he played along they'd leave faster than if he explained the whole thing was a mistake. Okay, not a mistake — a prank.

"Oh I almost forgot!" One of the guys held up a small noisemaker. The others, once they saw his, pulled out similar ones. They all blew on them, releasing a chorus of loud honks and streams of glittery confetti that exploded in the air around them.

Noah blinked as confetti streamed all over him. He watched as the men waved happily and then grabbed their clothes before filing out. A piece of confetti tickled the edge of his nose and he sneezed suddenly. When he opened his eyes, Jonas stood next to him, his hand covering his mouth.

"Don't even say it," he growled.

"I wasn't going to say anything." Jonas held his hands up in surrender.

Wordlessly, Noah walked over to the garbage can and brushed as much of the confetti off as possible. Glitter stuck to his shirt and hands, and he'd probably be washing it out until next week.

Jonas helped him gather the confetti streamers and stuffed them into the garbage can next to the conference table. Then he laughed suddenly. "I can't believe she got you a stripper-gram."

Noah had never been so pissed and simultaneously amused. How was it possible that he wanted to spank her and kiss her all at once? Actually he knew exactly how that was. The funniest part was that she'd no doubt thought the strippers would embarrass him in some way. Maybe she thought this would even the score between them, her embarrassment countered by his. It only showed how little she actually knew of him. You could only be embarrassed if you had any shame left.

He'd lost what little shame he had back on the streets.

"That girl has balls, that's for sure." Jonas handed over the folder he'd been carrying under his arm. "At least she's not pretending you don't exist anymore."

"I'm starting to think I'd prefer being invisible." Noah pretended he didn't see the look of pity Jonas threw his way. He definitely wasn't going there today.

Matthias stuck his head around the door. "Is it bloody safe to come in?"

Jonas snorted. "Scared of a few shlongs in thongs?"

Matthias's only response was the middle finger he waved in Jonas's direction. However, Noah noticed that he didn't say anything until Jonas left. It was rare for them to keep secrets from each other; after all, their safety often hinged on the entire group being fully apprised of every possible future scenario. Which meant something was up.

"What's wrong?"

Matthias shrugged. Then he glanced over his shoulder at the open door. "It's Lucia," he said in a low voice.

Fear lanced through Noah. "What do you mean? What's wrong with her?"

"Nothing. She's fine. Fuck, I probably shouldn't even be telling you this."

Noah took a deep breath and struggled to keep his temper under control. Raging at one of his best friends wouldn't help the situation. "If something's going on with Lucia then you need to tell me. I know you…care about her, too."

It was as close as they'd ever come to acknowledging their shared fate of loving a woman that neither of them had a chance with.

Matthias flushed. "I do. Care, I mean. And that's why I originally agreed to help her."

"Help her with what?"

Matthias pulled out his phone. A few thumb taps later he held it out so Noah could see the image on the screen. His blood went cold when he recognized the house.

"Where did you get that?"

His voice didn't even sound like his own, and he cleared his throat trying to get his composure back. But it was impossible to be unaffected when the past came back to haunt you. His time with ORUS wasn't something that he could ever forget, but he'd tried too damn hard to keep it in the past where it belonged.

Now it was rising like a specter to remind him that he'd never be free.

"Lucia asked me to help her do some research. She sent me a deed to a house and asked for info on finding the owners. All she had to go on was the name of the corporation on the deed."

"*Lucia* asked you about that house?"

Noah closed his eyes. This was so much worse than he'd thought. It wasn't just the past coming back to haunt him, it was the past reaching forward with icy fingers trying to snatch the only person he'd been able to save that day.

Matthias was watching him closely. "It's weird, too, because the name on the deed didn't actually match the corporation name. It's a fake. But I had the address so I could do some digging of my own. Then suddenly she said never mind. That she didn't need to know anymore."

"That's not like her."

"No, it's not. It's also not like her to ask me not to tell you about it. Which probably means she's doing something she shouldn't be."

Noah grunted. "She's mad at me right now."

"I figured that. But it's Lucia. She's always mad at you."

He shook his head. "Not like this."

Noah sighed. There really wasn't anything he could say to explain. He wasn't entirely sure what was different about this time. All he knew was Lucia was gone even while she was still there, and he'd never felt more empty.

When Noah didn't say anything, Matthias knocked on the edge of the table. "Mad or not, she's family."

Noah raised his head, the truth in Matthias's words ringing through his head. That day, that horrible day, had almost stolen everything from him, but he'd managed to keep the vow he'd sworn while bathed in blood. To pledge his life to Lucia and Nonna DeMarco. To protect Rafe's family.

To protect *his* family.

"Tell the others I'm taking the day off. I have to take care of something."

He was smiling.

Lucia closed her eyes, soaking up the late summer

rays and reveling in a rare afternoon spent with her ultra-serious big brother. Rafe was always lecturing her on how she needed to get better grades and work hard so she could take care of Nonna. He was always so serious but not today. For once, he was smiling and everything was wonderful.

A shot rang out.

Lucia flinched and then the scene shifted. Suddenly, she was in their car and Rafe was trying to leave her. Where was he going?

"Stay here. No matter what, okay?"

He always looked so fierce and serious. Lucia nodded, sure he was just being his usual overprotective self.

"Okay, fine. But really, where am I going to go?"

"I'm serious, Lulu."

He leaned over her and popped open the glove compartment. Lucia gasped at the sight of the gun and then went still when he picked up her hand and pressed the gun into her palm.

"Take this. If something happens… you drive out of here as fast as you can."

"Rafe, I can't drive yet."

"I've taught you enough. Just drive, Lu. As fast as you can."

A shot rang out.

"Rafe!"

She reached out for him but he was already falling. There was so much blood; it was on her hands, in her hair. Then she raised the gun in her hand and fired. And Rafe's body dissolved in her arms.

"I love you. Come back," she sobbed, trying desperately to hold on to his body but it flowed through her fingers like water.

A shot rang out.

Lucia bolted upright on the couch and then squeaked at the sound of a fist hitting the front door. It was hard to separate what was real from the dream, but as the knocking continued, she figured someone really wanted to talk to her.

"Okay, I'm coming." She pushed her hair out of her face irritably. She was still wearing her yoga clothes and hadn't showered. The damn dreams…It was getting harder and harder to sleep at night knowing what she'd see when she closed her eyes. So she'd been staying up later, reading, cleaning and just subsisting off of caffeine and adrenaline. It was finally catching up to her.

She leaned forward to check the peephole before opening the door. Noah stepped through as soon as the door opened, brushing past her and then closing and bolting the door behind him.

"Come on in. Make yourself at home," she grumbled.

"You don't get to be mad at me today. Not when I'm going to be washing glitter out of my ass crack for the next month after that little birthday production you ordered up for me."

The thought of Mr. Tough Guy finding glitter in unmentionable places made her feel a little better.

"Just a little payback. I hope you guys enjoyed the show, though."

Noah chuckled. "I don't know about that, but I was impressed at your creativity. It was just the right combination of cheerful and maddening."

"You taught me well."

Noah settled on the edge of the couch and leveled that stare at her. The one that always made her feel like she'd just been called to the principal's office.

"I did, which is why I want to know what the hell you're up to. Matthias told me about what you asked him to research."

Lucia's heart sank. "Bunch of tattletales you've got working for you."

He shrugged. "I think he wouldn't have told me except he says you called it off. Knowing how stubborn you are, he figured you wouldn't do that without good reason."

She kept her eyes on the floor.

"Lucia. If something happened, you need to tell me. Right now."

Her shoulders slumped. "Okay, but you have to promise not to freak."

"I think I can keep my head."

She walked back to her room and pulled the letter out of her night table drawer. It was still in the original envelope. When she got back to the living room, Noah was pacing in front of the window. Nothing was out of place, but she could tell he was on edge. Wordlessly, she handed him the envelope. He opened it and pulled out the sheet of paper. Instantly, it felt like the temperature in the room dropped twenty degrees.

Lucia had a feeling she was going to pay dearly for not showing this to him right away.

"When did this arrive?" he asked softly, his voice perfectly calm.

"Last week."

His only response was a soft grunt. "Last week. Of course it's been a *week*. Of course you've been walking around for a week with minimal protection and no regard for your own safety. *Of course*!"

He shouted the last two words and Lucia jumped. Then she backed up as he advanced on her, backing her against the wall, leaning over her until all that surrounded her was him. Instantly, her heartbeat accelerated and her stomach dropped. Noah would never hurt her, she had no doubt about that, but she'd never seen him quite like this. Wild. Untamed. Undone.

Captivating.

"You don't know how vital you are, do you? Not just to your friends and your family but to *me*. If something ever happened to you, Lucia…"

He dipped his head, his lips brushing against her hair. In that moment, everything inside her went liquid and she let out a soft sigh, suddenly aware that she'd been holding her breath the whole time. His scent was all around her and she wanted to rub up against him.

"Nothing is going to happen to me."

"You're damn right it's not. I won't let it. From now on, I'm not letting you out of my sight."

Ah, the man was infuriating. Lucia shoved him, annoyed that she could be so easily distracted by him when he was busy trying to take over her life. Again.

"I don't need a shadow. This is my problem and I've got it handled. You aren't my father, and I'm not a little girl who needs a babysitter."

He let out a low growl, the sound so insanely sexy that it brought a blush to her cheeks.

"Believe me, I know you aren't a little girl."

He tipped his head and their faces were so close...so close, that she could feel the warm whisper of his breath on her skin. Then suddenly he pulled her up on her toes and his mouth covered hers. His tongue slid into her mouth and over hers, making lust pierce through her.

She melted against him, her limbs turning to jelly. He kissed her until she couldn't think or move or even breathe. Her hands slid into his hair of their own volition, twining through the thick strands to hold him against her. He was her only anchor in a storm of sensation, and she hung on for dear life. By the time she had to break away to take a needed gasp of air, he allowed her to slide slowly down until she was standing on her own two feet again.

"I have to go, but I'll be back in a few hours."

"Why are you coming back?" Lucia barely recognized her own voice. That lazy, husky sound couldn't be coming from *her*, could it?

Noah tipped up her chin until she met his eyes.

"Because as of right now, you have a roommate. I'm moving in. I hope you don't snore, princess."

He left her standing against the wall in her living room trying to figure out how she'd lost complete control of the situation.

Chapter Six

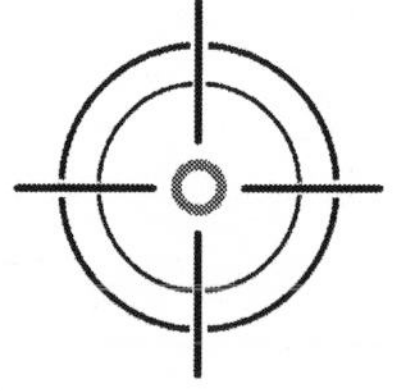

Noah staggered outside Lucia's apartment, slamming the door behind him.

Holy shit. What the hell just happened? One second, they were fighting, the next his lips were on hers and it felt like…bliss.

He was well aware of the location of the cameras, so

he waited until he was past the range of the camera right outside her door and before he was within range of the camera at the end of the hallway. His own personal blind spot. He leaned against the wall and tried to collect himself. The blood still rushed in his skull and her scent still permeated every cell of his body.

Fuck, he could barely stand.

What the hell had he been thinking? *You know what you were thinking.* He ignored the raging lust in his blood. For years, he'd managed to ignore the temptation. How he'd managed to ignore it for so long and then break it in one moment, one *ill-advised* moment, he had no idea.

This was a disaster.

He'd just been so *pissed*. It was a familiar feeling lately. He'd felt the same way watching her dating guys who weren't worthy of her. For once, it was time to get past the bullshit he'd been telling everyone for years about her being nothing more than a little sister to him.

He'd been *ill* watching her out on a date with another guy. He'd hated the fact that anyone else's hands were on her.

But it wasn't like he could have her himself. There would be no happy endings for the two of them. He was not the kind of guy she could take home to her family. Never mind that Nonna had practically helped to raise him, or had at least seen him into adulthood. That was hardly the point. She deserved someone way better than he was. She deserved a guy who would take her to church on Sundays, rub her feet on Wednesdays and make polite love to her on Fridays.

A guy who wasn't a killer.

A guy who wasn't so damn good at it.

He pushed away from the wall and inhaled a deep breath. He needed to get his shit together. First things first, he needed to make sure that Matthias scrubbed the surveillance footage of today. The last thing he needed was the guys giving him shit about this. He sure as hell didn't need Jonas with his knowing gaze tracking Noah's movements and his actions. He loved Jonas like a brother, but that shit was annoying.

He needed to sort this out and quick. Step one, keep Lucia safe. Her safety was all that mattered. Step two, never, *ever* kiss her again. How hard could that be? He'd managed not to touch her for years. He just had to remember all the reasons why he'd stayed away from her all this time.

Next, he needed to figure out who the hell had her in their sights. Because he may not have been able to save Rafe, but there was no way he was going to lose Lucia, too. She and Nonna were the only family he had. And he owed her.

He made the drive uptown back to the office in surprisingly little time. The moment he walked in the loft, he went straight for Matthias.

His shit-eating grin told Noah he'd already seen the video feed. Matthias winked at him. "I have always loved must-see TV."

Noah was in no mood. "I need you to scrub all the surveillance from Lucia's place today. All of it."

Matthias's brows drew down. "Noah, you set the rules. Standard procedure is we keep the footage for a month, and then we archive it. Just in case anything comes up. There might be something on there we may need later, especially given everything we know now."

Noah ground his teeth together, pretty sure he was going to crack a molar any second. "I said, clear the fucking footage."

Matthias stilled, and his eyes went wide. Noah saw that hint of fear, and it made his gut curl.

Even after everything, he couldn't escape what he was. No matter how far he'd come, he was still the thing that went bump in the night. His own men knew enough to be wary. Why didn't Lucia? How could she look at him with that sweet adoration and blind trust?

He forced himself to take a breath and relaxed his expression. He needed that footage gone, one way or another.

Matthias may have been a little afraid of him, but he wasn't backing down. "No. I'm not going to clear it, mate. I'll clear the segment of you and her in her place. But everything else stays." He shrugged. "Sorry, boss. They're your bloody rules."

The guy gave him a look that was all steady steel. And not for the first time, Noah was reminded of why he plucked Matthias out of ORUS with him when he left. There was a cold center to the kid that could come out when pushed, and Noah hadn't wanted that cold to grow and take him over completely.

Noah nodded. "Fine. Just erase that footage then."

Matthias nodded. "You got it." He hesitated. "But is now a good time to mention that Jonas has already seen it?"

Noah paused on the way to his quarters and muttered a string of expletives. "How the hell is that possible?"

Matthias shrugged. "Well, you were pretty pissed when you headed over there. None of us have ever seen you that angry before. He wanted to make sure you didn't kill her."

Noah turned to Matthias, working the muscles on his jaw. "I would *never* hurt Lucia."

Matthias grinned. "Oh we both know. We mostly wanted to see if you'd actually go through with it. For what it's worth, I said no way. Jonas made a cool twenty bucks off of me." He shrugged again. "That's what I get for loyalty."

Jesus Christ. Noah was going to kill Jonas. And then when he was done with Jonas, he was going to kill Matthias. Was it so obvious to everyone? How desperate he was for her? That he was fighting a losing battle with himself?

"Find Jonas. Tell him to get his ass to Lucia's until I can get there."

"He's already on his way."

Matthias was the only other one besides Noah who stayed at the loft. He hadn't wanted to at first, but Noah knew the big bosses at ORUS were less than pleased about losing their best hacker. He'd wanted to keep the kid safe.

Kind of like Rafe had done for him.

Noah had to remember though, that while Matthias might be young, he wasn't defenseless. The kid was good. Too good.

Kind of like Noah.

Besides, there was safety in numbers. The penthouse was a fortress. But one day, someone might come looking for them.

Noah shook his head. "Whatever." He padded across to his room, his angry stride eating up the concrete. When he reached his private quarters, he slammed the door behind him.

In the solace of his own space, he leaned against the door, his brain oh-so-helpfully replaying every moment of the last three hours. He needed to rewind. Go back to that moment before he kissed her. Because he was never going to survive if he kept thinking about it. So for now, he would just continue like he always had done.

Needing to work off some of the tension, he changed quickly and headed for the treadmill in the workout room. After forty-five minutes of a grueling pace, he hopped in the shower, not allowing himself to linger. Routine. That was what he needed.

Once showered, he finally paid attention to the grumbling in his stomach. Unfortunately, when he opened the freezer, there were signs of Lucia everywhere. All the food she'd brought over. She knew he was useless in the kitchen. Lasagna. Wedding soup. He spent a good deal of his time deliberately making her crazy, but still she took care of him. Because that's what you did for family. And like it or not, Lucia was his family. He would do whatever was necessary to protect her, even from himself.

Noah snapped open his laptop to pull down the status reports from each of their open jobs. But he couldn't find the dongle for his wireless mouse. With a groan, he pushed himself back to his feet and went to the bedroom to retrieve it. When he opened the drawer beside his bed, his heart stopped. Right under the dongle, sat a photo of him, Lucia, Rafe, and Nonna. It had been taken nine months before Rafe died. They looked happy. They looked like family. Back then, he'd been too young to know what he was getting himself into.

Too young to know what he was doing to his soul.

With a curse, he shut the drawer on his past, the guilt gnawing at him. Because of him and his choices, his ego, his friend was dead. If he couldn't forgive himself, how could he ever expect Lucia to? No. She was better off with someone else. Someone who wouldn't get her killed. He knew what he had to do. Protect her with his life and keep his hands off of her.

Resolutely, he pulled out a bag to pack.

Noah Blake was simply the most infuriating man Lucia had ever met. How dare he think he could just dictate her life?

Infuriating. Annoying. Bossy. So damn bossy. And Jesus Christ could the man kiss. He'd left over thirty minutes ago, and she still couldn't calm her heart rate. Thinking about Noah crashing his lips to hers as he backed her up against the wall made her ache in places. Ache and *tingle*. Because while something low in her belly pulled at her center, her nipples peaked. Her skin itched, as if it was too tight over her muscles. And her lips, well, she wasn't talking to them.

Who are you kidding? It was the best kiss you've ever had in your life. That was what was missing from her date with Brent. That was what was missing with every guy she ever attempted to date. That heat, lust, longing, need. All of those things.

But why, why did it have to be Noah? She always pictured herself dating a great guy, the kind of person she could bring home to Nonna, but who still also made her feel tingly all over. The kind of guy who wanted to go and meet her friends and hang out having picnics in Bryant Park.

Yes, she maybe watched and read one too many romantic comedies. But that was beside the point. She wanted a *normal* dating life. Where she would call some guy, chat for hours, and then argue about who would hang up first. Wasn't that how it was supposed to go? JJ was her only real marker for these kinds of things, and JJ was more of the 'play hard to get and then screw the guy senseless before leaving him wanting more' kind of girl.

Lucia couldn't do that. And dammit, Noah was all wrong. There was always an edge to him. A hint of danger.

Rafe had been his mentor of sorts where they worked. Back then, she'd been completely dazzled because he was the only one who had the nerve to swear in front of her. And, he was older, so yeah, of course there was an inappropriate crush.

But she was older now. She got it. She understood that guys with edge, guys with hidden tattoos, who rode motorcycles and checked every movement with their shrewd eyes, those guys were dangerous.

Those were the kind of guys that had killed her brother. She wanted nothing to do with that type of man. Especially not now. She'd been serious when she said she was going to back off. It wasn't worth her life. Rafe wouldn't want that. But that didn't mean she didn't feel the pull to Noah like the gravitational force of the sun. Every time she was in a room with him, she couldn't help but track his movements, be aware of him.

Did he feel the same way she did? As she struggled to pin down exactly how she felt, something caught her eye on her coffee table. Noah had left his damn phone. And someone was leaving a message.

Probably one of his many women. Did they know he was busy kissing her? Okay, she needed to stop thinking about that kiss. Because every time she did, her body betrayed her.

She picked up his phone and saw the notification.

ALARM: All secure. Movement in living room.

She stared at the message. What the hell? The rational part of her brain tried to reason with the irrational suspicion bubbling in her blood. *It can't be what you think.* No. It couldn't be what she thought. As she stared at the phone, she knew she was about to cross a line. She'd seen Noah enter his password so many times that she knew it by heart but entering it now would be breaching his trust. Then the phone flashed with another notification.

Oh hell. Lucia entered the code and then gaped at the picture that had just come in. A clear image of her damn living room.

Lucia dropped the phone. She did a quick circle around the room. Holy hell. He had cameras in here? Throughout her house? She shuddered. Sometimes she understood why he was so protective of her, but to have a surveillance camera in her damn house? She was going to kill him.

Her brain scrambled to come to grips with the messages she'd just seen. Murder was the only solution. That was the end of that. She'd hated violence ever since Rafe had been taken from her, but this required bodily harm.

Take a deep breath. Remember what he taught you. Be systematic. She'd always thought Noah was being crazy when he taught her to look for bugs and was hyper about her security; when he'd taught her to put a little piece of tape up above the door so she would know if someone had come into her place unannounced. Even if they hadn't touched anything.

He taught her all sorts of ways to be sure she was safe. Except she wasn't safe from him. She stared at her front door, checking the doorframes and the peephole. After that, she systematically moved to the walls. She checked all the picture frames, picking them up off their hangings, inspecting the frame, looking for anything that could be a camera or that looked 'off.' One by one, she rehung the pictures and then moved over into the living room to the bookcase. After a thorough scan, she found what she was looking for. Right dead-center of her bookcase, was the picture frame Noah had given her for Christmas last year. In it, she'd put a picture of her, Noah and Nonna from Christmas breakfast that morning.

In the picture, her grandmother was squeezing her tight, leaning up to give her a kiss on the cheek. On her other side stood Noah, smiling but somehow a bit separate in the image. He was somehow always there, always a part of her family. But not really. All this time, how long had he been watching her? And why? It was time for some damn answers.

But first, she was going to find the rest of it. She wanted all the surveillance gone. She knew everyone thought she was so innocent and needed to be sheltered. She might not know exactly what Noah did, but she knew the kind of man he was. Protective. Strong. But this? She stared down at the picture. This was going too far. She spent the next hour meticulously searching her house. She didn't want to tamper with the security system in case that was actually necessary. But the moment he was back, she would have him remove anything that was in there.

After a thorough sweep, she found two bugs and two cameras, both sets in the living room and kitchen. Luckily, there were none in her bedroom. Thank God, but that didn't let Noah off the hook. He was going too far. She knew he felt like he had to take care of her after Rafe died, but this…this was another level. She wasn't going to stand for it. As soon as he got back, he was going to give her some answers.

Chapter Seven

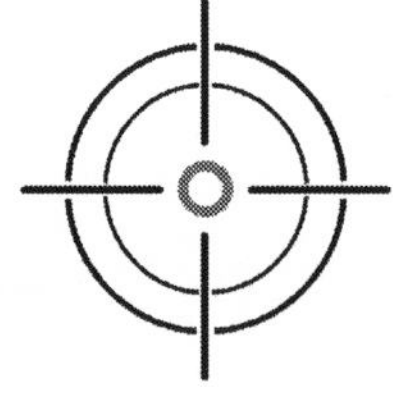

Matthias stopped in his doorway. "Boss, have you heard from Lucia?"

Noah stopped in the middle of shoving clothes in a bag to glare at Matthias. "What the fuck are you talking about? You saw me get kicked out of her place not two hours ago. Speaking of which, is Jonas there?"

Matthias licked his lips. "Yeah, he's there, but listen, something's up with her."

"What's wrong?"

Matthias shrugged. "I'm not sure."

"What do you mean?"

"She's being weird."

Noah finally lost his patience. "What the hell does that mean? What is she doing?"

It took a moment, but Matthias finally said, "Not sure. She's moving things around. I guess she's redecorating but it's really difficult to see what's going on. There's all this crap in front of the camera now."

Noah's mild panic started to recede slightly. "You're sure Jonas is outside?"

"Yeah, of course. He just checked in, right on schedule. I don't know, something just seemed off. It might be nothing, but I figured you'd want to know before you walk into that."

Noah finished grabbing underwear and a few toiletries before tossing his shaving kit on top of it all. "You know how she is. Antsy when she's annoyed. I'll fix it when I get back over there."

It took Noah much longer to get his things than he'd anticipated. By the time he got back to Lucia's apartment it was almost midnight. Luckily, Jonas had been able to stick around and keep an eye on things until he could get back. Moving in with Lucia sounded easy enough in theory. But once he'd started packing up, it had become clear just how much stuff he relied on every day.

The thought brought to mind *the people* he relied on every day. Maybe by the time he went in to work tomorrow he'd have figured out what he was going to say to explain his new living situation. Matthias already knew, of course, since he was usually the one monitoring Lucia's surveillance feed. But he could already hear the bullshit he'd get from Jonas when he found out.

That was the problem with hiring your friends. They knew you too well for you to bullshit them, and they always had something to say about what you were doing. Especially since they knew what Lucia meant to him. It wasn't something he'd ever admitted aloud, but it was one of those things that was so obvious it didn't require explanation.

He knocked and shifted his duffle bag to the other shoulder. While he waited, he looked up and down the hallway. Most of Lucia's neighbors were older, one of the main reasons they'd gotten her into this building. The location wasn't exactly convenient to his office, but a longer commute time was no big thing in the long run.

It would be no small feat to run his business from another location, but there was no doubt in his mind this was the right move. The *only* move. Lucia was more important than anything else. There weren't too many things in his life that he'd gotten completely right, but taking care of her and Nonna DeMarco were at the top of his list.

He could only hope that if Rafe was looking down

on them, he'd be proud.

Noah wasn't a religious man, despite Nonna's best efforts, but he took his oaths seriously. He'd promised Rafe that he'd take care of them if the worst ever happened, and he'd lay down his life to keep that vow. Especially since his best friend couldn't have known that the worst thing out there was Noah.

He knocked on the door again and then stood back so Lucia could see him through the peephole. She'd gotten much better about not opening the door without checking first. It had killed him that living in this neighborhood had made her soft for a while. After a few minutes of standing there, he started to get impatient. He let his duffle bag fall to the ground. There was a dull clank as all the electronics jostled against each other. He'd probably brought more tech gadgets than clothes.

"Lucia, open up!"

There was no sound inside. Noah frowned. Jonas would have let him know if she'd left. She'd been pissed at him earlier but it wasn't like her to be petty. She was way more likely to open the door and yell at him than leave him outside making a scene in her hallway.

He knocked once more for good measure and then pulled out his key. Once inside, he disabled the alarm. As soon as he flipped on the lights, his hand instinctively went to the Sig Sauer holstered on his hip.

What the hell?

The place looked like it had been trashed. Every

couch cushion was on the floor, and the chairs had been knocked over. The bookshelves were swept clean, the books and knickknacks littering the floor. His blood went cold as he realized that something was very wrong. There was no way this kind of mayhem could have occurred without their surveillance picking it up. If someone had circumvented their security measures then he had no idea what he was walking in to.

A soft sound drew his attention, and he walked quickly and quietly down the hall to Lucia's bedroom door. It was quiet, but then he heard her voice. She was on the phone. She didn't sound upset or even frightened. Confused, he pushed the door open.

Lucia was reclining on the bed with one hand under her head and her phone in the other. The only light in the room came from the small lamp she'd left on next to the bed. A single picture frame rested on the comforter next to her. The picture frame that he'd given her for her birthday last year.

The frame that housed a pinhole camera. It sat next to his phone. He must have left it behind.

Lucia mumbled something and then put the phone on the bedside table. He holstered his weapon.

"Is everything okay?"

She gave him a murderous look. "What do you think?"

He wasn't sure how to answer. Maybe it was a coincidence that she had that particular frame out. "Were you doing some redecorating?"

"Seriously? That's all you have to say to me?" She gestured to the frame on the bed next to her.

Noah hung his head. "Fuck."

"You have some serious explaining to do."

Lucia watched warily as Noah moved closer. Her friends would probably describe her as calm, levelheaded and in control, which made the feelings of rage swirling inside her even harder to take. When she'd found the camera, it was like a switch had been flipped and a new, never-before-seen side of her emerged.

Over the years, she'd tolerated a lot from Noah. He thought she didn't understand him, but she truly did. He'd been her brother's friend, protégé, and more like family than anyone else in their life. So even though he'd never spoken about *that day* with her, she already knew why he worked so hard to take care of her and Nonna.

Rafe had been extremely protective of the women in his life, and she had no doubt that somewhere along the way, he'd tasked Noah with watching over them if he wasn't around to do it himself.

Only someone who'd known her brother would

understand just how hard it was not to give in when Rafe wanted something. Even when she'd been a young teenager and chafing under the supervision of her extremely chauvinistic big brother, she'd had a hard time being mad at him. There had just been something about Rafe that made you want to let him handle things. He'd had that sort of aura, the kind that made you want to trust in his leadership and work extra hard to make him proud.

So she got it. She understood.

But there was a line that had been crossed somewhere along the way, and Noah seemed to have forgotten that not only did he have a responsibility to Rafe, but one to her as well. She was the one he talked to every day. Rafe had been his best friend, but she was one of his best friends now. Or so she'd thought.

Because a friend wouldn't do this to her. A friend wouldn't violate her privacy without a second thought.

"I guess I don't have to ask if you know what that is." Noah gestured toward the picture frame resting on the comforter between them.

"Since you're the one who taught me how to spot a pinhole camera, no, you don't. My question is, when did you switch the frames?"

Although she asked the question casually, Lucia was truly interested in the answer. The camera hadn't been there when she'd gotten the frame. She would have noticed it. Which meant he'd waited until she was used to seeing the frame on the shelf and then swapped in a dupe at some point. It was clever, and damn if that didn't make it all worse. Noah was brilliant and diabolical. Traits that she'd never thought he'd use against her.

"I waited until Easter."

She shook her head, furious when tears sprang to her eyes. "Nice long game. So you've been spying on me ever since. Funny if I hadn't seen the text alert on your phone, I never would have known."

He ran a hand over his hair, tugging at the dark strands in frustration. She'd never seen him look this unsettled.

"You don't understand, Lucia. If something ever happened to you…this was for your protection."

"What are you so worried about? What aren't you telling me?"

For a moment he stared at her and she thought, *finally he'll confide in me*. There were so many moments when she could tell he was holding back, and all she wanted was to be the one person in his life he didn't keep secrets from.

"Nothing. I just want you to be safe," he finally said.

The same standard answer he always gave when she asked why he was so hyper-vigilant about her security. The disappointment covered Lucia like a blanket. In that moment she realized it was never going to happen. He would never trust her or see her as anything but someone to protect. Never a partner, never his equal, and certainly never his soul mate.

The loss hit her all at once, and suddenly she was as

heartbroken as she was furious.

She stood up and went into her closet. When she came out holding her suitcase, Noah's eyes flared with anger. He grabbed it from her.

"Why do you have your suitcase? You're not going *anywhere* right now. I know you're mad at me, but we have bigger things to worry about right now. Like whoever wrote that note."

Furious, she tugged on the handle until he let go. She suspected she only got it away from him because he was surprised she'd fought back. She'd barely gotten it open before he was right there zipping it back up.

"Get out of the way, Noah! You can't tell me what to do. You're *not* my boyfriend. One kiss doesn't give you the right to interfere in my life."

"What about two kisses? Does that give me any rights?"

He stepped in front of her, blocking her access to the suitcase, and all the blood left her head. Lucia swayed, and of course the bastard used that as an opportunity to pull her against his chest. For a moment she rested there, taking in the scent that was uniquely his and the sultry, sandalwood notes in the aftershave he'd used for years. It would be so easy to forgive him and let him cajole her into submission. But that wouldn't change anything. He'd still see her as an obligation, and she'd still be pining for something that could never be.

She pushed away from him, fighting against his hold when he tried to keep her in his arms.

"You wish. You're lucky you got one kiss. And it wasn't even that good!" She added that last part in a rush of anger, hoping to make him feel as unsettled as she did.

Got him, she thought, watching his eyes narrow at the insult.

"I'm pretty sure you were into it at the time. Want an instant replay?"

Before she could process his words, his hand slid up her back and under her ponytail, holding her still. His lips covered hers and Lucia froze in place. It was just as explosive as the first time, as everything female in her responded to the dominant way he took what he wanted. Lucia gasped and when her lips parted, and his tongue slid against hers in an erotic dance that made her even more lightheaded.

Her entire universe contracted to that moment; her body pressed against the muscular frame that had haunted her dreams for years while the man she loved desperately kissed her stupid.

Noah slid one leg between hers, and the contact of his hard thigh against her core made her cry out. She'd never known she could feel like this; hot and cold, furious and elated, damned and blessed, simultaneously.

"That's it, princess. God, you're so perfect. Everything I should never touch." His whispered words didn't even make sense in the moment, but the soft rasp of his breath against her neck as he kissed his way down her throat sent her soaring.

Lucia's eyes opened briefly, and while he was busy doing things that felt amazing to her collarbone, her eyes landed on the picture frame on the bed.

Noah had never said these sorts of things to her before, and *she knew him*. She knew how he operated. Everything she'd discovered today had proven that he'd use any skills he had to get his way.

Even seduction.

She shoved him away and then picked up the frame from the bed. He ducked just in time to avoid getting clipped in the forehead when she threw it at him.

"You aren't going to distract me by pretending to want me, Noah."

He blinked at her, his eyes looking lazy and seductive, the way she'd imagined he'd look when he woke up. Or after lovemaking. Lucia shook her head, trying to clear her mind.

"You think I was pretending?"

Noah looked down, and Lucia followed his gaze to the huge bulge in the front of his jeans. *Oh my god*. Her breath left her lungs in a rush.

"It doesn't change anything," she protested weakly.

Noah walked forward and she tensed, worried that if he kissed her again she wouldn't have the willpower to resist a second time.

"It changes everything, princess."

He leaned forward and Lucia closed her eyes, bracing for another erotic assault. Then her eyes popped open at the gentle kiss on her forehead.

"Go to sleep. Before I give you what your eyes are asking for."

She watched as he strode out of the room, pulling her door closed behind him.

Chapter Eight

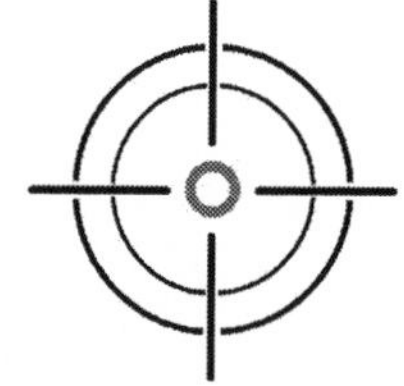

Do not think about Lucia.

Do not think about Lucia lying naked in bed.

Not that Noah knew whether Lucia slept naked or not, but either way, it didn't matter to his dick. Damn thing hadn't gone down since he'd gotten a taste of her.

He was such an idiot. He should have never kissed

her. Because once that line was crossed, there was no going back. No pretending. She'd been there, she'd felt the desperation he had to keep touching her, to keep holding her, pressing his body into hers. It was unmistakable. His only option right now was to attempt to bring them back to normal. To before.

His dick twitched against his thigh as if to say, *yeah, good luck with that*. He groaned and turned onto his side, flipping the pillow under his head. Problem was, as big as the couch was, it was still just a smidge too short. His feet were dangling off the edge. The blanket he'd pulled out of the linen closet covered his feet but not all of his chest. And dammit, *he* usually slept naked. Somehow, he didn't think that was going to fly with Lucia in the next room. Noah rolled over again and stared at the ceiling.

How did you end up here?

Because you insisted you knew best.

He'd intruded on her privacy. He knew it. And the thing was, he wasn't sorry. He'd been keeping watch over her for years. Keeping her safe. Keeping her from finding out about ORUS. About Rafe. About himself. Allowing her to keep her air of innocence for as long as possible. Allowing her to live the kind of life that was only possible when you were oblivious.

But now, when there might be real danger, he had no idea how the hell he was going to keep her safe. He had no idea why she had started digging into Rafe's death again. Or maybe she'd never stopped wanting answers. He wasn't even sure exactly what she'd found. Suddenly her date with Brent made sense. Whatever she'd asked the pencil pusher to look up, someone didn't want her asking questions about it.

He had Matthias digging for any traces of that company name she'd given him, but so far he hadn't found anything. He just prayed that whatever she was doing, he could still keep her safe. She was messing in some dangerous waters, and he couldn't let her get too close to the man that he'd been before. Because then she would be in real danger.

Noah considered all the things he'd kept from her for years. How would she react if she knew the truth? If she was pissed off now, he could only imagine how she would feel about him then. She would run out of his life and never look back.

He shook his head as if he could dislodge the unsettling thought. He couldn't allow that to ever happen. If she knew what he was, the kind of man he was, *the things he'd done*, she would never speak to him again. She would never even look at him. Right now, she was mad. She was pissed off. But she would eventually see that he had her best interest at heart.

If she found out the truth, it would be over.

There would be no more family dinners at the DeMarco house anymore. No welcoming arms, even when she was irritated with him. It would be over. The one constant in his life since he was fifteen, gone.

After what he'd done, he deserved worse. But he didn't want to lose her. That could never happen. He wouldn't *let* it happen.

In a perfect world, one where he wasn't a natural born killer, he could have a girl like that. Sweet. Sunshine practically pouring out of her. A completely normal life filled with all those silly things that couples did. Brunches at Bryant Park, walks around the city talking about nothing, horseback riding in Central Park. All that stuff he'd always seen as cheesy and stupid. But cheesy or not, they were things he would never have. That was family. That was love.

That's not for you.

No. He knew that. He'd learned that lesson a long time ago.

From her bedroom, he heard a low buzzing noise, kind of like her phone was ringing. He immediately rolled over to his side, and picked up his phone off of her coffee table. He'd paired their phones together. Yes, without her knowledge, but it was for her own good. Whatever, he'd eat guilt on this one. But there were no incoming calls, or text messages. What the hell?

When he rolled back to his side and his dick dropped again, he suddenly had a very good idea of exactly what she was doing in there. And it made his blood run hot. His muscles bunched as he tried to force his brain to think of anything other than Lucia using that monster dildo on herself. Legs splayed wide, eyes rolled back in her head, panting.

No. Stop it now.

He couldn't have her, so he wasn't thinking about her like that. That was just a recipe for —*Jesus Christ.* The buzzing was still going on.

With a growl, he called out, "You'd better not be using that monster vibrator in there. You know I can hear it."

Immediately the buzzing stopped. She was silent. Quiet as a church mouse. Her happy drawer went against everything in his mind of exactly who Lucia was. The problem was that in a twisted way, that knowledge only made her way more interesting. And even more damn untouchable. With a frustrated moan, he sat up.

"Hey, DeMarco. Just wondering, does that thing stand up and tap dance too? Inquiring minds and all that."

Yeah, he was giving her shit. Being an asshole. But he needed her to stop using that thing. It was bad enough he kept thinking of all the myriad ways he could use it on her. Those dirty thoughts weren't going to help either of them sleep.

He called out again. "What's the matter? Pussy got your tongue?"

Shit. His brain was working against him. Now all he could do was think about his tongue on her p—never mind all that.

"You know, I hear you can go blind if you use those things too much."

Noah lay back against the pillow and smiled into the darkness when he heard one of her drawers slam shut.

If he wasn't getting any sleep tonight because of his

raging erection, then neither was she.

Number of attempted orgasms: 1.

Number of setting changes on battery-operated boyfriend: 4.

Number of hours of sleep obtained: 0.

Number of attempts to stop thinking about Noah: Infinite.

Lucia had slept like a monkey's ass, and her mood was not made any better by Noah with his tight-shirted workout that morning. She managed to stumble out of her room, bleary-eyed and in desperate need of coffee, only to find him in work out gear doing push-ups in her living room. Beads of sweat clung to his hair and his muscles were clearly defined under his clothes. And the worst part was, he looked—delicious.

There, she said it. He looked amazing. Sweat had molded the T-shirt to his ridiculous body. She may or may not have spent a good couple of minutes counting his abs. Or licking them in her mind.

No. Stop it. Noah is the devil. She hated him. Okay, so not exactly *hated,* but he pissed her off like no other.

And infuriatingly, the asshole totally caught her staring. Like a man with too much sex appeal for his own good, he'd given her one of his shameless cocky grins. As if to say, 'Yeah, I know what I look like. Were you dreaming about this last night?'

She'd have had no other choice but to say 'Hell yes.' She *had* been thinking about him. And no, it hadn't gotten her anywhere. Except to Frustration City.

By the time she made it into the office after being jostled on the subway for thirty minutes, she was ready to rip someone's head off. This morning, Matthias had been her escort, and he'd been perturbed at her refusal to get into the SUV. But he'd had no choice but to follow her onto the subway. After all, what was he going to do, throw her over his shoulder? First, he wasn't the type. Unlike the others who worked at Blake Security, he wasn't a caveman. She wondered about him sometimes. There was no way Noah would have sent him with her if he didn't know how to protect her.

Luckily, JJ was the first person in her shoebox of an office. Her best friend was guaranteed to put a smile on her face.

"Morning sunshine. You excited? I'm so stoked about my first fashion week. I know you've been to a couple of these now with Adriana, but I can't wait. I get to sit in on the final strategy meeting for hair and make-up. I guess you're getting the final model list today?"

Lucia got it. JJ was excited. After fashion school, JJ had been apprenticed to a makeup artist. Lucia had managed to score a gig here at Adriana Patterson Fashions. When JJ had been looking for change, Lucia recommended her. It was awesome getting to work with her best friend, but not first thing in the morning before her second cup of coffee and after a night of no sleep. JJ was just far too chipper for eight o'clock in the morning.

"Yeah, sounds great."

"What's up? You're extra grumpy today."

The guilt hit Lucia hard. "Sorry. It's not your fault. It's freaking Noah."

JJ sat on the edge of her desk. "What? The strippers were a perfect idea. Did they not show?"

Lucia groaned. "Oh, they showed all right. Noah was *pissed*. And the company sent me a video recording of them singing happy birthday. I have digital proof of Noah at the center of a confetti storm. That part is awesome. What's not so awesome is Noah in overprotective mode."

JJ laughed. "What? Did he decide that you are somehow dating one of the strippers, and he wanted you for himself?"

Lucia rolled her eyes and shook her head. "That's not why he does those things. He thinks he's protecting me. What he's really doing is being an ass. I don't have a father or big brother anymore. I don't need him volunteering."

JJ sighed. "I have told you a million times that Noah isn't volunteering as tribute. He does this shit because he wants you. Sooner or later you're going to need to see that. But I digress. What's his problem this time?"

Lucia checked the time and stood. "I need to go get Adriana's coffee. Walk with me and I'll fill you in?"

"Yep, let me get my purse."

They headed out of the building toward the heart of Soho. Adriana had a very specific coffee order that only one coffee cart vendor in the city carried. And he didn't open until 8:30. So this was part of the routine. What was *not* part of the routine was JJ peppering questions about what Noah was doing at her place. Or the shadow she knew had to be following her.

"Okay, you know how I've been looking into the situation around how Rafe died?"

JJ nodded. "Yeah, I remember you said that you might've found out who owned the house right? That was Brent right? The records guy? He gave you the information."

Lucia nodded. "Yeah, he gave me what I was looking for, and I sent it off to Matthias to look into on the lowdown for me. But then a couple of days later, I got a letter in the mail telling me to stop digging."

JJ stopped dead in her tracks. "Excuse me? And is there a reason you don't have an armed escort right now? Why aren't the cops following you around? You know, skulking behind corners trying to act like hidden bodyguards? Ooh, even better, a young Kevin Costner?"

Lucia dragged her along. "I swear to God you sound just like him. I don't *need* a bodyguard. Anyway, once Noah found out that I'd asked Matthias for help and then got this note, he insisted that he was moving in. So, there he was this morning, working out or whatever, and looking hot in a T-shirt."

JJ grinned. "Oh, I see. You're getting a little hot and bothered under that buttoned up collar. That's totally normal. And you realize he's doing it on purpose right?"

Lucia frowned. "What?"

"Honey, the guy has a gym at his place. As if he needs to work out in your tiny ass living room. Besides, if he's so worried about you, why didn't he send you with an armed guard to protect your ass?"

Lucia groaned. "Who says he didn't?"

They slowed as they reached the coffee cart and took their place in line. She angled her head to the northwest where a black SUV sat, with Jonas in the driver's seat. He winked at her.

She rolled her eyes and turned back to JJ. "Jonas is on duty this morning. He's been following us since we left the office. Matthias accompanied me on the subway because I refused to sit with Jonas in the car. So I do have armed bodyguards. I just don't want them."

JJ laughed. "Somehow, this is not the hot sexy bodyguard scenario I was picturing in my head. I mean, they are sexy as hell, but I was picturing more of you and Noah in a forced proximity kind of thing."

Lucia rolled her eyes.

"So, what are you going to do? I mean are you going to stop looking into Rafe's death?"

Lucia shrugged. "Right now I don't really feel like I have a choice. Noah could help. He has resources. But he doesn't want me digging into any of that stuff. Keeps telling me if I go digging, I might find things I don't want to know."

"Maybe he has a point, sweetie."

"How can he say that to me? To be quiet and not worry my pretty little head? At the same time, whatever my brother was working on, he was killed because of it. I still have nightmares. So for now, I'm letting it go. Because all I've ever wanted is normalcy. And if someone doesn't want me to look, it may be a good idea to lay low for a while."

JJ's eyes went wide. "So you're listening to Noah for once?"

Lucia smacked her friend on the arm. "If you tell him, I swear to God I will shave you bald."

JJ laughed. "Whatever. I could totally pull off a pixie cut. Okay, look. Maybe you need a night out to forget about all this stuff for a bit."

"How? I'm not going to be allowed to go anywhere without my oversized baboons following me. They'll never let me out of their sight. Let alone go somewhere that's going to be hyper crowded. They'll probably escort me right back to my place tonight. No detours allowed."

JJ scoffed. "C'mon, it's Friday night. And I feel all right."

Lucia laughed "I wish. But even if I could shake them, they have this uncanny way of always finding me. They're probably tracking my phone."

JJ chewed her bottom lip as she thought it through. "Well, what if you left your phone here? You don't need it while you're with me. I have my phone. If anything weird happens, you can call Noah. He may not be too thrilled, but you're still perfectly safe with me."

Lucia considered the idea. Noah would be pissed. But he had bugged her place, so he deserved to have her give him a hard time.

"Okay, let's say we do it. Exactly how am I supposed to ditch Thing One and Thing Two? I see Jonas. But I know Matthias is around here somewhere. I just can't see him."

JJ laughed. "You leave that to me."

Lucia lifted her brow. "Why do I have a feeling that we're going to get in trouble for this?"

"Oh, ye of little faith. You know the girl in Accounting, the one with the curly hair? She matches you enough in looks and height that if you change clothes, they'll follow her back to your place. Or at the very least follow her onto the subway. Which is just enough time for us to get into a cab and go party."

Lucia stared at JJ. She'd always loved her friend's more adventurous side, but this…this was diabolical. "You think it'll work?"

JJ gave her brisk nod. "Noah and crew will never know what hit them."

Chapter Nine

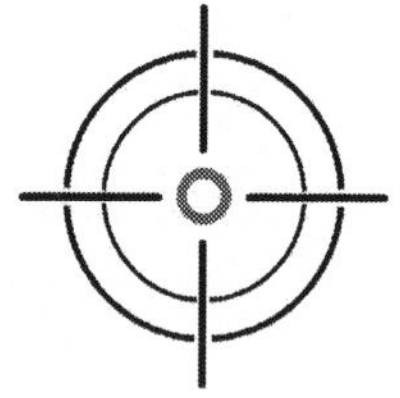

Lucia tossed back her first and only shot of the night and wiggled her hips to the techno beat blaring through the club. This wasn't usually her scene, but after how tense everything had been, she had to admit that JJ was right. Alcohol and dancing were the cure for almost anything.

"Are you having fun?" JJ yelled over the music. As usual, her friend looked amazing, even while sweaty and tired.

Lucia pushed back a curl that had escaped from the high bun she'd eventually pulled her hair into. No matter how she started the night her hair always ended up in a bun. It was the only way to contain the frizz.

"I am. This is exactly what I needed," she yelled back.

JJ smiled but her eyes kept going to something over Lucia's shoulder. She turned and saw a tall, well-built blond guy near the bar who was staring at JJ.

"That guy is cute. You should go talk to him."

JJ shrugged. "Maybe later. Gotta make him work for it." But even as she said the words, her eyes slid back over to the bar.

Suddenly, Lucia realized why her friend was being so nonchalant. She wasn't much for clubbing, but even she knew the rules. You don't ditch your friends for a guy unless you're sure they'll be okay without you. Since it was just the two of them, JJ wasn't going to leave her alone. Which made her feel guilty. Just because she had no sex life, it didn't mean that her friends should have to suffer.

"Go talk to him. I'm fine. Actually I'm going to head out anyway."

"Are you sure?" JJ bit her lip and glanced back over at the bar. Lucia turned around too and then laughed when the guy winked at her friend.

"Yes, I'm sure. Go!" She pushed JJ in his direction and then grabbed the small clutch she'd abandoned on top of the table when they started doing shots. She watched wistfully as JJ approached the bar and climbed onto the stool next to blondie.

She'd give anything to have her friend's confidence but truthfully, it probably wouldn't even matter if she did. Her heart had been lost years ago to a grumpy, overbearing asshole she'd never have. On that depressing thought, she walked down the stairs separating the bar area from the main dance floor. The club was packed and before long Lucia was overheated and slightly nauseous from being bounced between all the people.

Suddenly, someone grabbed her from behind. Lucia twisted frantically and screeched as adrenaline flooded her system. But in the midst of the crowded dance floor it was impossible to move away.

"Get your hands off me!"

The music was so loud that no one paid any attention as she was picked up and carried through the crowd. She went slack, forcing her attacker to carry the full brunt of her body weight. To her surprise, he just turned her around and threw her over his shoulder. She got only a glimpse of Noah's pissed off expression before she found herself hanging upside down.

Shock made her compliant. How the hell had he found her?

Finally they reached a dark part of the club. Noah set her gently on her feet and put his arms on the wall on either side of her to keep her from escaping.

"How did you know where I was?"

Noah glowered at her. "I have my ways. What the

hell is wrong with you, Lulu? Do you think this is a game?"

His use of her old nickname sent shock through her system. No one had called her that in a very long time. Not since Rafe died.

"I'm not playing games. I'm just trying to live my life. A life that doesn't include you."

"Is that really what you want?"

"No. None of this is what I want. What I want is for my big brother to be alive and for him to be here annoying me right now instead of you. So go away and leave me alone."

"That's not the world we live in. And since we don't live in fantasyland, there is no way that I'm going to leave you alone, ever. I failed him but I will not fail you."

"What does that mean?"

Noah sighed and bowed his head. He wasn't going to tell her. It always came back to this, his inability to let her in.

He moved to block her when she tried to walk away but at her evil glare, he allowed her to pass. It took quite a bit of maneuvering to get to the door past all the sweaty, moving bodies, and she had no doubt that Noah's hulking presence behind her was the only thing that got most of the people to move. *What a metaphor for the rest of my life*, she thought with amusement. Noah had always been like that, largely unseen in the background of her life until she needed him.

Outside, she took a big gulp of fresh air. It occurred

to her that this was the perfect time to make a run for it. If she surprised him, there was a chance she could catch a cab and get in before he could catch up. As if he could guess her thoughts, he leaned over and whispered "Don't even think about running."

"There you are! I saw you get grabbed…" JJ suddenly appeared on the sidewalk next to her. "Oh, it's you." She looked between them with a knowing smirk on her face. "Hi, Noah."

Noah nodded in her direction. "Hi, JJ. Do you need a ride home?"

"No, I'm good. There's a sexy Viking inside who's going to plunder my spoils tonight. But thanks."

Noah grimaced, unsettled as always by JJ's bluntness. "Great."

JJ was aware that she wasn't his favorite person, and it had never bothered her. Instead she took the opportunity to needle him every chance she could.

"Heard you've been playing with dildos. I can get you one of your own if you want."

"No, that won't be necessary." Noah looked almost green now.

"Okay, if you're sure. I get a discount so it's no biggie. Hope you enjoyed the stripper-gram the other day. That was my idea."

Lucia snorted behind her hand, the events of the week and the long night of dancing suddenly catching up with her. The street swam before her and she would have fallen over if Noah hadn't caught her.

"And that's our cue to get home." Noah flagged down a passing cab. JJ stood back as he bent and scooped Lucia into his arms.

"Wait. Noah, she was really hurt by whatever happened between you guys earlier. Will you…just be careful with her, okay?"

"I would never do anything to hurt her."

Then it occurred to Lucia that JJ didn't know that she'd been drinking virgin margaritas all night. She probably thought Lucia was drunk. Lucia almost lifted her head to tell them both she could take care of herself but then stopped.

She was finally where she'd always longed to be. In Noah's arms.

Her heart pounded so hard it felt like it was trying to escape her body as she curled her fingers in the front of his shirt, wishing she had the right to do this all the time. But for now all she could do was rest her head on his shoulder and absorb the feeling of being safe and secure in his arms.

Anything else would have to wait.

The ride home seemed to take forever. The entire time, Noah looked down at the sleeping angel in his arms and wished that things could be different.

Lucia deserved the kind of guy that could be honest with her and tell her his darkest secrets. Share everything. But that would never happen. His darkest secrets would break her, and that was the absolute last thing he would ever want to do.

The cab pulled up outside her building, and Noah shifted slightly to pull out his wallet. He handed over a few bills, not even caring if he'd overpaid. All of his attention was on taking care of Lucia. He'd never seen her the way she'd been tonight. For an hour, he'd stood in the shadows watching as she drank and danced and looked more lost by the minute. Maybe no one else would have been able to tell, but he could see the sadness in her eyes and it killed him to know he'd put it there.

He'd broken her trust, and he'd do it over and over again. There was no possible happy ending to this scenario. She'd only be hurt more deeply the closer she got to him.

Lucia stirred only when he had to set her on her feet to open her apartment door. Even then, she leaned against him, almost melting into him, looking up at him with achingly big gray eyes.

"It's okay, princess. We're home."

As he whispered the words, he'd never wished more intensely that they could be true. That this could be *his* home and that he could belong there. It had been so long since he'd had a true home.

She closed her eyes and leaned against him again as he carried her inside. Noah didn't bother with the lights since he knew every inch of her apartment just as well as he knew his own place. He settled Lucia on the couch and shrugged out of his jacket. After a moment of hesitation, he took his holster off as well. He was going to have to wake her to get some water in her and she hated to see his gun, always had.

He walked into the kitchen and retrieved a bottle of water from the fridge. After opening it, he took a swig himself. Even though he hadn't been drinking, he'd spent an hour sweating bullets wondering where she was before finally tracking her through JJ's phone. He wasn't sure if Matthias had done something illegal to find out where she was, and he wouldn't be asking.

He walked back into the living room and knelt next to the couch where Lucia had burrowed into the pillows.

"Lucia? I need you to drink some water."

She sat up slightly and took a few sips. Her eyes stayed on him the whole time. After draining about half of the bottle, she set it aside.

"Let's get you into bed."

She shook her head. "Not yet."

Noah swallowed hard as he watched her. She was so damn beautiful. The curtains had been left open and moonlight illuminated the living room. There were several shoes kicked off by the door, like she'd had trouble deciding which ones to wear that morning.

He eased her onto the couch and pulled a throw over her. Unable to help himself, he watched her sleeping for a moment. If he could he'd memorize the lines of her face and the adorable way she moved her lips while she slept, like her mind didn't stop working, even in sleep.

When she suddenly opened her eyes, he wasn't ready for it. They stared at each other, naked emotion on display for a few seconds before she shocked the hell out of him by tugging on his hand until he sat on the couch next to her. She scooted over to make room for him.

"How do you do it?"

Her voice was soft in the quiet of the room but still penetrated all the way to the deepest part of him.

"What?" he asked gruffly.

"How do you live without knowing why?"

Surprised to see her eyes wide open and completely alert, Noah wasn't prepared for her to ask *that*. "That's not really a middle of the night conversation, princess. Go to sleep. You'll feel better in the morning."

Lucia sat up in bed and crossed her arms. "I'm not drunk, Noah. I was drinking virgin drinks all night."

"I saw you do a shot."

"Yeah. *A* shot. As in…one. I was able to fool JJ into thinking I was partying before that but then she wanted to do shots. I couldn't really ask the bartender for a shot of apple juice."

Noah laughed. "Why do you hang out with her, anyway?"

At that, Lucia glared at him from the corner of her eye. "Maybe she's loud and brash and occasionally pushes me to do things outside my comfort zone but you know what else she is? *Honest*. With JJ, what you see is what you get. She would never lie to me. That's just not how she rolls."

Noah closed his eyes. "I know you're still angry with me."

She had every right to be pissed at him but it wouldn't change anything. He still couldn't confide in her, and he was still going to annoy the hell out of her by hovering.

"I miss him so much."

When he looked at her again, Noah was shocked to see tears streaming down her cheeks. Lucia was an emotional person but carried herself with such dignity. He'd only seen her cry the day of Rafe's funeral. She'd put on a stoic face as she consoled her grandmother that terrible day and every day since. But apparently Lucia was as skilled at hiding her true feelings as he was.

Moved by her emotion, he moved closer and gently thumbed away the tears. She sighed and pressed her cheek into the palm of his hand, and Noah knew with certainty that he'd never love anyone else quite like this.

"I miss him too, princess. Every fucking day. I'm always thinking about what he'd do in a situation or what he'd say if he were here."

She looked at him pleadingly. "How do I let this go? If I stop looking for answers, it feels like I'm letting him down. Because he'd never stop searching for justice for me. Never. Even if he was afraid of what he'd find."

Not caring that this was far too intimate, Noah pulled her to him. Lucia let out a sob and clung to him, her arms wrapped around his neck so tight he almost couldn't breathe. He welcomed the discomfort. He'd take any pain for her. Anything but telling her the truth that would devastate her so completely.

"I can't stand to see you cry," he whispered.

Lucia glanced up at him and then slowly raised her hand to his cheek. He was shocked when she drew it back and her fingers were wet.

"I don't want you to be hurt either," Lucia said. Then she curled her hand behind his neck and tugged him closer.

He should have pulled back. He should have turned away. But, the only thing he could do in that moment was allow her to guide his lips to hers. The first brush of their lips sent a shock through Noah that jolted him to the core. The kiss was soft, sweet, and it filled Noah with a sense of rightness that he'd never felt before. This woman was his sun, his sky, and his reason for existence.

"I love you, Noah." Her whispered words sent him soaring, and then just as quickly, crashing again.

She couldn't love him. She didn't truly know him. If she did, she wouldn't be looking at him with her heart in her lovely gray eyes. A good guy would tell her that, turn her away. Protect her from himself.

Then Lucia smiled and kissed him again, and he was lost.

Chapter Ten

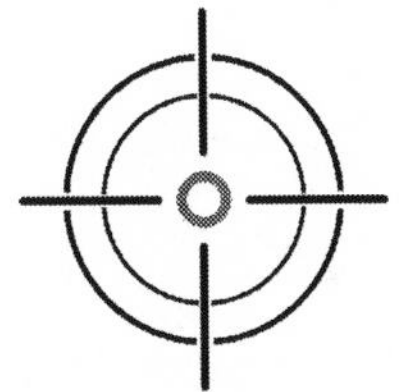

"Lucia?" he murmured against her lips.

Lucia stared up at Noah. He was asking permission. Or maybe he was asking if she'd lost her damn mind. She wasn't sure. All she knew was that she wanted his lips back on hers. She didn't want him seeing her as a little sister. Not anymore.

She reached up and cupped his cheek gently before sliding her hands into his hair and pulling him to down towards her. As he leaned over her, she could see the torment in his eyes, the confusion. As if he waged a war with himself.

She had no clue what she was doing. All Lucia knew was that she liked this feeling. This tingly, too-hot, desperate feeling. She liked being in his arms. She didn't know what that meant, but she didn't want him to stop.

He growled low in his throat and Lucia was no longer in control of the kiss. His lips crashed on hers, pouring heat and desperation and desire into her with every lick of his tongue into her mouth, with every graze of his teeth on her lower lip.

Noah angled their bodies, until she lay back against the arm of the couch. As they shifted to get more comfortable, he moved so that he partially lay over her, his full weight resting between her thighs.

Oh God. Yes, please.

His lips were expert. Equal parts gentle, but demanding, coaxing a response out of her with his tongue, with his hands, which teased at the hem of her T-shirt.

His thumbs gently grazed her skin in slow circles. All Lucia could do was hold on and dig her hands into his hair. He slid his hand further under her T-shirt, teasing the lower ribs, making her tingle.

Involuntarily, Lucia raised her hips in a desperate attempt to get closer to him. Before she knew what was happening, his strong hands picked her up and over, lifting her until she straddled him, bringing her center right onto his —

Oh. My. God. He is huge.

And that felt—amazing. His hands gently gripped her hips as he kissed her, rocked her over him. The motion made her cry out.

Noah dragged his lips off of hers, kissing along her cheek and then her jaw. His hands were in her hair, tugging her head back, exposing her throat. He brushed his lips against her throat, murmuring, "You are so fucking beautiful."

She felt beautiful in his arms. Sexy. Wanted. Lucia rocked over him again, his strong hands guiding her, showing her exactly how to move. He nipped at her throat, gentle love bites, followed by teasing licks to soothe the tiny wounds.

Lucia tried desperately to drag air into her lungs but all that came out were tiny pants, hardly enough to stay conscious. Screw it. Who needed consciousness? She loved this buzzing, floaty state with Noah. This alternate world. One in which she was sexy and he wanted her more than his next breath. She didn't want to go back to reality. Not yet. She just needed—more.

Noah dragged his lips away from her throat, and somewhere in the room there was a low whimpering sound. Wait, was that her?

Noah chuckled. "So you want more do you?"

He took her hands, and slid them over his

shoulders, into his hair before bringing his lips back to hers; giving her those heady kisses that put her brain into a coma and made her heart thump and her body tingle.

As he kissed her, his hands slid up under her T-shirt again. And when his thumbs grazed the undersides of her breasts, Lucia gasped, automatically arching into the caress. Against her lips, she could feel his smile. He knew exactly what he was doing, how he was making her feel. And she didn't care, she wanted more.

"I think we can get rid of this," he whispered.

Lucia looked down at the T-shirt he tugged on, and she nodded her head briskly. "Yeah. Who needs this old thing?"

He gave her a lopsided smile as he tugged on the hem. She raised her hands to make things easier for him, and up and over it went, making barely a sound as it hit the coffee table behind her.

Noah stared, his eyes pinned on her bra as he licked his bottom lip. Impatient, she rolled her hips again, riding along the edge of his erection, and his gaze snapped back to hers. "You feel what you're doing to me without even trying?"

Breathlessly she asked, "Am I doing anything?"

He gave her another patented Noah Blake grin as his hands slid up her back to support her. He leaned into her, gently kissing along her ribs on the left, and then across to the other side. Kissing the underside of her bra, and then her sternum. Teasing. Promising, but not delivering. Driving her crazy. He was doing this on purpose. He knew the effect he had on her. Knew that any second, she was going to burst into flames.

"Noah—"

"Easy, princess. No way in hell I'm rushing this."

Damn it. She needed—more.

Through her bra, Noah blew a hot breath directly on her nipple. That tore a low moan out of her chest. *Holy cow. That was so—*

But he wasn't done yet. With one thumb, he drew gentle circles over the opposite nipple, even as he wrapped his lips around the now hardened bud. He grazed gently with his teeth, then lapped at her with his tongue.

"Oh my God. Jesus."

Behind her, his fingers flicked and she felt her bra strap release. The next thing Lucia knew, his mouth was on her. *Hot. Wet. Slick.* With every pull of his tongue and lips, her core contracted. She involuntarily rolled her hips, seeking more contact, more friction, just *more.*

Apparently, Noah had plans to torture her as he moved to do the exact same thing to her other nipple. With an expert flick of his tongue, pulling and tugging, he made her beg.

Noah Blake completely owned her body.

With his lips still around her nipple, he made a muffled sound as his fingers slid down her ribs, and her torso, past her bellybutton to where she rode him. Oh so gently, he ran his thumb over the heat of her core through her leggings, and she bucked.

With a hand firmly on her ass, he kept her in position and continued to tease her with his teeth. His thumb drove her closer and closer to the edge of bliss and destruction. One stroke up, one stroke down, then a slow, teasing circle.

Ooh God, she was going to die like this—hovering on the edge, not knowing what it would feel like to—suddenly her body bucked and shook, and stars exploded around her. The rush of heat and heaven and pure pleasure flooded her bloodstream.

"Oh my God, Noah."

Against her nipple, Noah muttered, "Yeah, princess. That's it. Let go for me."

Lucia thought he might stop, but he kept up the onslaught, dragging her right back up the mountain only to push her over once more. When another wave of pure bliss washed over her, she sagged.

Noah finally let up with his thumb. He gently released her nipple and kissed up to her collarbone, then her jaw, and gently kissed her lips. "My God, I love how you do that."

Lucia flushed. "I don't think I've ever—"

But she didn't get to finish, because Noah was kissing her again. Gentle, unhurried, but deep. Against her core, his erection still throbbed as if begging, 'I'm still here. Please don't forget about me.' Not that she could.

He gently lifted her so that her legs wrapped around him, and he carried her through the living room and down the hall to her bedroom.

He gently set her down on the bed before reaching for her leggings and dragging them off in one fell swoop. Then he reached behind his back and dragged his T-shirt over his head. With only moonlight streaming in through the edges of the blinds, all she could do was make out the shape of his broad shoulders and the ridges of his abdominal muscles.

Holy hell. He was—wow. She held her breath and waited for him to finish undressing. Geez, they were really doing this. And despite the fact that she'd never done it before, she wasn't scared. Quite the opposite. She wasn't worried at all.

Except, well, he was huge. But she wanted him. She wanted *this*. She'd wanted Noah Blake from the moment she'd first noticed boys, so there was no stopping this train. She was running past go, and she was going to collect her $200.

Noah undid his buckle, shoved his jeans down and stepped out of them easily. Before he tossed them though, he reached into a pocket and grabbed his wallet, taking out a condom and tucking it into the back of his boxer briefs.

Noah climbed on the bed beside her and tugged her to him, pulling her body flush against him, and the hair on his chest made her nipples tingle with awareness again. He flipped them over so that she lay on top of him.

Against the juncture of her thighs, his erection pulsed, begging for freedom. Lucia brushed her fingertips along his stomach, his muscles bunching and shifting with every trace.

When she reached the edge of his boxers, Noah dragged his lips from hers and cursed. "Lucia?" he asked, his voice gravelly as she teased her fingertips along the edge. When his hips rose, he muttered a string of things he'd never said around her before.

"Yes, Noah."

His breath hitched. "You know you're driving me crazy, right?"

She was driving *him* crazy? She was the one who felt like she was on the edge of desperation. Now she wanted to play a little. "Am I?"

Another hip roll from him. "Yes. You can't tell?" His voice was barely audible as his muscles tensed.

She lifted her head to watch him carefully as she traced her finger over the soft cotton to the bridge of his erection. Deliberately, she traced her fingers along the length of him. Noah hissed, but he didn't stop her. She grew bolder, wrapping her fingers around him and squeezing gently. Wanting more, she released him and then slipped her hand into his waistband.

Noah sat up. "Lucia, wait."

She froze. "Am I doing it wrong?"

He gave her a sharp chuckle even as his brows furrowed down. "Wrong? Fuck no. But if you—"

She wrapped her fingers around him again, feeling the softness of his skin, the throbbing pulse as the blood that ran through his body concentrated in one organ. Gently she pumped him, fascinated that she was having this kind of effect on him.

"Oh, *fuck*, Lucia. Jesus. I won't make it. You have to—"

Lucia traced her fingers to the tip, spreading the drop of moisture that had pooled. "Is this okay?"

Noah groaned but didn't stop her. Instead, he dug his hands into his hair and tugged while he let her play. His body twitched and bucked under her exploration. But he didn't push, nor did he stop her. Lucia raised her gaze to meet his. He was watching her with a half-lidded look of desperation in his eyes. She turned her attention back to what she was doing. Her tongue snaked out of her mouth as she wondered what those pearly drops of moisture tasted like. She licked her lips.

Noah cursed. "Oh, no you don't. If you put your mouth on me, I'm not going to make it. And I think I owe you at least a couple more orgasms before you put me down for the night."

She had no idea what he meant, but damn he was fast. Before she knew it, he had her flat on her back with his lips on hers again. With both her hands safely trapped in one of his, he kissed her deeply. When he pulled back, he nipped at her bottom lip.

"I think that's enough playing for now. You can play more later. Right now I'm too on edge."

He took the sting out of taking her new favorite toy away by giving her something he knew she liked. He lowered his head to her nipple, sucking, licking, driving her back to that brink of heaven. But this time, instead of just stroking her through her underwear, he took his hand down to the juncture of her thighs, parting her gently.

Lucia had to remind herself to breathe, trying to remember how to do the simple motion she did every day, all day. It was too difficult with Noah teasing her. In and out.

Noah teased the skin where the elastic of her underwear met her thigh and then nudged the fabric aside. His thumb found her slick, wet, and one of his fingers gently teased her entrance, probing, testing.

Against her breasts, he muttered, "Fuck. I could do this all day." And then he slid a finger in deep.

Lucia never stood a chance…especially when he curled the finger inside her, pressing gently.

Holy Mother of God. He pressed again gently stroking back and forth, and then she was sailing over the cliff, happy to dive without a parachute. Her body quaked, tightening around his finger, desperate to hold it inside.

"Oh my God, Noah."

He hooked his thumbs in the elastic of her panties and tugged them down easily. And then, he splayed her hips wide with his broad shoulders, tucking his hands under her ass, lifting her to him. The first stroke of his tongue made her moan. He stroked her again and again, and soon one orgasm rolled into another, and she had no idea where Noah ended and she began.

With every stroke, lick, gentle flick of his finger, and penetration of his tongue, she was flying into the void.

She collapsed against the pillows, her body limp, unable to move. Noah kissed his way up her thigh even as he chuckled. He rolled away to shuck his boxers. Then she heard the tearing of foil. When he rolled back, he settled over her. She lifted her hips impatiently.

"Lucia, you're supposed to let me take my time."

No way that was happening. She lifted her hips again. She wanted him. She wanted this. He was taking too long.

Noah growled deeply before sinking in to the hilt. She hissed. *Oh God.*

Noah muttered, "Fuck. You're so tight."

"Noah—"

He pulled back a little, and Lucia wrapped her legs around his back. No way was he leaving. He dropped his head to her throat and nuzzled her gently as he sank back in. Another curse.

He repeated the action, small movements, until the sting and burn were replaced with something far more intense, far more pleasurable. Once again, Noah was dragging her to the edge of the cliff, but this wasn't a race for something fast and fleeting like a flash of fireworks. This was stronger, more tangible somehow.

Noah dropped his forehead to hers. Her fingernails dug into his shoulders, and she blinked rapidly as she tried to hold on tight. His gaze met hers and held. Then he made love to her. His hips rocking in and out; slide, retreat, slide, retreat, never breaking eye contact.

She matched him thrust for thrust, rocking her hips into his, seeking more contact. Her fingers clutched desperately at his shoulders, trying to pull him deeper. "Noah, please," she whispered.

Something broke, and it was like the tether on his control snapped. He rocked into her again, harder this time, his pace increasing. No longer gentle, he bit his lower lip and his motions became more desperate. His hand tightened on her hip, almost bruising.

His lips were a demand on hers, his hand in her hair under the nape, angling her so he could kiss her deeper. And then it happened again. Lucia broke all the way down to her soul, and she squeezed her legs around him, unwilling to let go as her body convulsed.

"Jesus, what the fuck...Fuck me." His pace increased, almost punishing, he was no longer in control. He was chasing her. Chasing bliss. Chasing something more.

When he came, his body went rigid over hers and he threw his head back as he roared. Lucia dug her nails into his shoulders, and he gripped her tight.

And as she looked up at him, she knew she would never be able to get him out of her blood.

A faint sound from the other room woke Noah with

a start. He reached for his gun holster and realized he'd left it in the living room with his phone. He was used to being ready for action at a moment's notice. One damn night with Lucia and he was forgetting critical shit?

Rookie mistake, dumbass.

The phone chimed two more times, and then after a brief pause, started again. He had to get that. Lucia's body curled into his side. The sheet had slipped, exposing her bare shoulders, and he wanted to kiss one of the freckles he saw there. But if he did, he'd want to kiss more. And if he was right, his old life was calling.

Noah slipped out of bed without waking her, quickly padding into the other room to grab his phone before the noise woke Lucia. He entered his passcode and then stared at the string of text messages he'd just received. To anyone else they'd look like a string of random letters and numbers, but to Noah, they were a reminder that his past was never too far away.

What the hell did Ian want? The series of messages told him who the anonymous caller would be. It was a system they'd worked out at ORUS. A series of secure text messages sent through relays, pinging across several countries. They'd learned every agent's signal as a matter of course.

Three minutes later when the phone rang from a blocked number, he answered, "Ian, what's wrong?"

Ian's voice was mellow, calm. But then, that was Ian for you. Nothing ever ruffled the guy. Not the years of wet work. Not the time he'd almost bled out in an alley with no help for three days, save a scared sixteen-year-old kid.

Ian didn't particularly seem to enjoy his job either, but that didn't make the dude any less eerie.

"Noah, you sound well. You almost sound like you were sleeping."

Noah ran a hand over his hair as he stood naked in Lucia's living room, talking to a ghost. "Well, I sleep much better now but you know the drill. I still never sleep through the night. Too many ghosts. What do you want, Ian?"

His old friend hesitated a moment, and that pause made the hairs on Noah's arms tingle. Something was very, very wrong. Ian didn't hesitate about shit.

"Look, I'm calling out of respect. For you. For Rafe."

Fuck. "Spit it out, Ian."

"There's been a call put out for a job. It was assigned to me, but I'm feeling a little sluggish today. I don't really know if I want to get out of bed for anything less than 200K. So a job like this, no skin off my back to give you a call and a heads up."

Noah's skin went cold, clammy. They were finally coming for him. After two years, they were pissed enough to come for Matthias? That was the only thing he'd done to truly piss off their superiors. He'd known the kind of people he had worked for. It had been a risk taking the kid, but he'd had to. Besides, ORUS were supposed to be the good guys…as assassins went. They only went after the worst of the worst. The ones who had managed to evade local and international laws. The things that went bump in the night. Why were they coming after him now? Why did what he'd done to free Matthias matter after two years?

He was so lost in thought, he almost missed what Ian said next. "It's the girl. We got a call out for Lucia."

Noah's whole world stood still as the icy tundra pushed away all warmth, all feeling, all sunshine. "What the fuck?"

"Job came in about thirty minutes ago, right before I texted you. So it's fresh."

“What the fuck happened to you guys being the good guys?”

“*You* guys?” Ian asked incredulously. “You forget, once you're one of us, you stay one of us.”

Noah's chest constricted as he looked towards the bedroom. If they were coming for Lucia, they'd have a hell of a time getting through him first. He needed to get her to the office. The place was a fortress. Except, shit. He didn't want her scared. Didn't want her paralyzed with fear.

Fuck. They needed a plan. For starters, no way was she going anywhere without an armed guard. Probably two. Fuck it, three. Noah dragged his attention back to Ian.

"Why call me? You know how that will look. And do you want to fucking explain to me how taking her out is for the greater good?"

There was another brief hesitation before Ian answered. "Let's just say I'm keeping to the respect thing. Besides, I don't think you were wrong for leaving. ORUS, what we do here, it's not for everyone. But we are concerned with the greater good, even if you don't see it. The kid, she's turning up stones that will get a mess of people killed."

"Did you send the letter?" Noah demanded.

There was a pause. "What letter?"

"She got a letter a couple of days ago that told her to stop digging. You guys fucking with unarmed civilians now?"

"I know nothing about it. Look, if you can keep her safe, and you can get her to stop looking, maybe this shit goes away. Either that, or you take her and the money you have squirreled away and you run."

"I'm not fucking running." That came out as more of a growl.

Ian sighed. "I know. It was worth a shot. If you want, I can find out more about exactly who wants the hit. I'll try and keep it discreet. Orion's still salty about Matthias."

"Thanks, Ian. I owe you one. After the way I left…" He let his voice trail.

Ian cleared his throat. "You saved my life once. Besides, you saw a way to save your soul and you took it. I can't be mad about that. Someone like me, I'm too far gone, if I ever had a chance in the first place."

Noah had to get the fuck out of here. He had work to do. "Any way you can buy us a day or two?"

"Not likely. Orion makes sure there are fail-safes on each job. Since you. Since Rafe. Not much chance of holding him off. But I'll see what I can do." His old friend took a deep breath. "Look man, watch your six."

"Will do." Noah hung up from Ian and immediately called Oskar to come and take guard watch. Then he began snatching his clothes off of Lucia's bedroom floor like a co-ed at a frat party. He spared her only a small glimpse before leaving. He'd fucked up last night. Gotten way too close.

She was a bright ray of sunshine, and he, well, he was all darkness and shadows. He may not be worthy of her, given his past, but he could sure as shit protect her.

And he would do that with his life.

Chapter Eleven

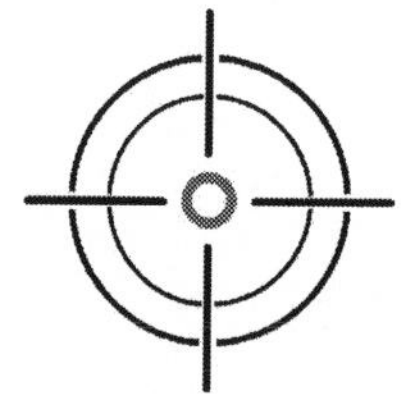

Lucia's eyes flew open and for a moment, she didn't know where she was. The sound of a gunshot echoed in her head. She shivered and her fingers curled around her comforter, clenching the fabric so hard it hurt. As her eyes adjusted to the darkness, the dream receded and the panic that had put her heart in her throat faded a bit.

She was home, safe in bed.

With a soft moan, she buried her face in her pillow, grateful tears welling in her eyes.

Breathe in. Breathe out.

She focused on slowing her breathing until she was calm enough to open her eyes again. It took a few seconds for them to adjust to the darkness, but then she was able to pick out the shape of the table next to the bed and the chair by the window where she always threw clothes when she was deciding what to wear. It was comforting to focus on the familiar shapes that told her she was home. Not back in the courtyard of an unfamiliar building with her brother's dead body on the ground next to her.

She sat up, dragging the sheet up and around her shoulders. The nightmares were becoming more frequent. Before this week, it had been a few months since the last one. Was it really accurate to call it a nightmare when it had really happened? It was more like her memories deciding to torment her. If she concentrated hard enough, she could feel the cold weight of steel in her hand and the blast of pure rage that had fueled her as she pulled the trigger. Certain details were so vivid it was like a painting she could reach out and touch. But no matter how hard she tried, she couldn't see his face, her brother's killer. The man she'd shot in a rage, desperate to protect her brother and herself.

Thinking about that always led her down a rabbit hole of depression that took weeks to crawl out of. After years of self-reflection and a short bout of therapy, she'd learned that it was best to stay positive. She'd lost her brother but Lucia had survived. There was nothing to be gained from lamenting the way things had happened in the past when she couldn't change it.

Lucia had long ago learned that staying in bed staring at the ceiling after a nightmare didn't help her fall asleep so she decided to go watch a movie in the living room. When she tried to stand she sucked in a sharp breath.

"Oh, whoa."

Moving slowly, she sat back down on the edge of the bed. The dull throbbing between her legs brought back the more recent memories of what had happened right here in this very room. The fact that she was completely nude was also a dead giveaway. She'd slept with Noah. How could she have forgotten? Only a nightmare could have distracted her from the most monumental event of her adult life.

She smiled remembering how wild and passionate Noah had been and how…*intense* it had been to be completely one with him. It had been overwhelming but in the best way.

"Noah?"

She waited to see if he was in the bathroom or perhaps had gone to the kitchen to get a drink. When there was no reply, she stood again, dragging the sheet around her naked body like a toga. The hallway was dark but she could make her way from memory. She flipped on the light in the kitchen. It was empty. She got a glass down from the cupboard and filled it at the sink. After taking a drink she walked into the living room.

Where the hell was he?

Lucia swallowed against a rising tide of panic. He wouldn't just leave her after last night, would he? She curled a hand around her neck and rubbed the knot of tension at the base of her nape. Maybe he was walking around outside just to make sure they were safe. She opened the door and poked her head out in the hallway.

One of the bodyguards Noah had hired last year stood across the hall. She had only seen him around the office sporadically but thought his name was David. Or was it Derek?

He straightened up, and then his eyes slowly widened as he took in what she was wearing.

"Um, hi. Did you need anything?" He asked while keeping his eyes somewhere over her left shoulder.

Lucia blushed so hard it felt like her cheeks were melting. When she glanced down she almost choked as she realized that her toga-style sheet had slipped and was exposing an extreme amount of cleavage. Freaking perfect. No wonder the poor guy was so uncomfortable.

She was going to kill Noah for this.

"No, I don't need anything. Sorry about...well, whatever. See you later...Derek?"

"It's Dylan," he said with a small smile.

"Right. Dylan. Well, see you around."

She backed up and then closed the door, careful not to catch her sheet. The last thing she needed was a wardrobe malfunction. They'd both spontaneously combust from mortification.

She stood there for a moment, unsure of what to do. Noah had left. He'd just…left. What did that mean? Things had been so great, hadn't they? At least they had been for her. Maybe it wasn't good for him?

Feeling completely lost, she walked back to her room and picked up her cellphone. Then put it back down. She wasn't going to be some needy girl who called him crying because he'd slept with her and then bailed before she woke up. She was a modern, independent woman and she could handle this. He was the one missing out because she was *awesome*.

Lucia climbed in bed with the sheet still wrapped around her and snuggled beneath the covers, an angry tear escaping. A few seconds later her hand shot out and grabbed her phone. It only rang twice before JJ answered in a sleepy voice.

"Hello?"

"It's me. I slept with Noah last night and then he was gone when I woke up. What does that mean?"

There was a pause before JJ answered. "*Motherfucker*. I'm coming over."

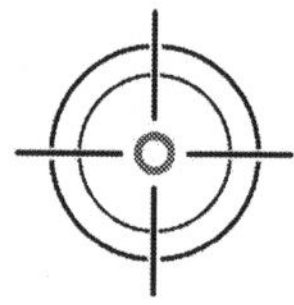

"Knock knock. Is it safe to come in?"

Noah looked up to find Jonas standing just outside. Normally he would have just barged right on in. Any of them would. But everyone had been giving him a wide berth that morning. He was as prickly as a bear and starting to get on his own nerves.

"Come in."

He waved a hand absently for Jonas to take a seat in one of the modernistic metal chairs in front of his desk. Everything in the office had been designed to be efficient, functional and easy to clean. That was exactly what he'd wanted at the time, but in his current mood, the stark atmosphere wasn't helping any. That was one of the side effects of spending the night wrapped up in Lucia's softness. It had been like ascending to heaven, only to be dropped back into hell a few hours later.

How was he supposed to walk around in the world after an experience like that? She'd been so sweet and so damn eager to please. Noah gripped the paper in his hand, no longer able to see any of the words on the page. All he could see was Lucia's lush curls tangled on her pillowcase, the hesitant but trusting expression in her beautiful eyes when she'd taken him deep for the first time.

That look in her eyes had smashed him over the head at about five o'clock this morning. He'd been in the middle of rearranging the caseload for the next month so he could have all available agents covering Lucia. One minute he was seeing the scheduling system on the computer. The next, all he could see was her beautiful face and that damn look of blind trust and love.

"Damn, you have it even worse than I thought," Jonas muttered.

Noah looked up to find his friend watching him with a mixture of pity and disgust.

"Don't even say it."

"Fuck that. I'm the only one who has the balls to come in here and confront you, but somebody has to. What the hell are you doing, man?"

The softly spoken question hit the target, making Noah feel even more like shit than his own conscience had been able to. Worst of all, he had no answer. There was nothing he could say in his own defense.

"This is not the time, Jonas. I know I fucked up. Believe me, I am fully aware."

"Are you really? Because if you don't want us all up in your business, maybe you should have Matthias kill the video feed beforehand."

Noah groaned and pressed the heel of his hands against his temples. He regretted reinstalling the camera over Lucia's door. He'd been singularly focused last night, first on getting Lucia home safe and then protecting her from the newest threat. Nowhere in all of that had he even considered that the entire team would witness the aftermath of his monumentally bad decision-making.

"Fucking hell," he muttered.

"Luckily, we couldn't see that part," Jonas said. "But we all saw Lucia wandering around this morning wearing nothing but a sheet. We all saw her face as she was looking for you and finally realized that you weren't there."

It broke Noah to imagine his sweet princess waking up to discover that he was gone. For her to have to face the fact that she'd given herself to the worst sort of man. All those guys he'd driven off, and he'd been unable to protect her from the worst predator of all. *Himself.*

Jonas seemed to sense Noah's inner torment because he slid forward in the seat, his face softening a little. "Look, everyone knows how you feel about her."

Noah squeezed his eyes shut. "You don't know shit."

"I don't want to see you mess up a good thing," Jonas continued, as if he hadn't heard the bullshit coming out of Noah's mouth. "Stop being a dick. Lucia loves you, too. We can all see it. Don't push her away out of fear."

Anger rose up in Noah, blinding him with its ferocity. Did they think he didn't want to be the kind of man that deserved a woman like Lucia? He would give his left nut and probably the right one, too, for even a shot at making her happy. But wanting something didn't make it possible, and there was no amount of redemption that could ever clean his slate. There was nothing he could do to come back from where he'd been, and he would never expose the purest, brightest thing in his life to that kind of darkness.

He owed her that, at least.

"Let's be real here. She is…perfect. I'm not going to pretend I don't want her. A dead man would rise up from the grave for a chance to be with her. But you know who I am, Jonas."

Noah held the other man's gaze until his friend dropped his eyes with a defeated sigh. Jonas stood, and after a moment, put a hand on Noah's shoulder. The touch would have pissed him off coming from anyone else, but the warm weight that only a decades-long friendship could bring was much appreciated right then.

"I know you feel like you don't deserve her. I get it. But you are the only one she has left, too. Are you really going to trust her safety to someone else?"

After he was gone, Noah dropped his head to the back of his chair. Jonas could give him all the pep talks in the world and feed him a bunch of kumbaya bullshit all day. But in the end, they both knew what kind of depravity lurked beneath the surface of Noah's skin. They'd both witnessed what it was like when Noah lost his veneer of civility and returned to his roots. And what was in him was not pretty. It was not civilized.

Would Lucia look at him with those trusting eyes if she knew how many lives he'd taken? Could she hold him close at night knowing that she was nurturing a man who could torture another without losing a wink of sleep? As a young boy, Noah had learned that the parents he adored had died, and since then he hadn't had the luxury of emotions or weakness. He'd never even wanted them because in his world, staying alive was the difference between caring too much or not at all.

All this self-reflection wasn't changing a thing. He'd fucked up by getting involved with Lucia. She'd be angry with him for a while, rightfully so, but that didn't change his conviction to protect her. All he could hope was that he hadn't hurt her too much.

The look of trust in her eyes flashed through his mind again. Then Noah sat straight up as something occurred to him. Something he hadn't thought of this entire time and should have.

Lucia was a sweet girl. Shy. Quiet. For years, she'd lived under her grandmother's roof, and for years after that he'd scared off any guy who tried to get close to her. Noah prided himself on his attention to detail, so the fact that he could have missed something so monumental was unbelievable. But all the signs were there, plain as day.

"She is never going to forgive this." He dropped his head into his hands.

How the hell had he missed the fact that she was a virgin?

Chapter Twelve

Yeah okay, Noah knew he had fucked up.

After Jonas had read him the riot act, he'd had hours for regret to come crashing down on him. How the hell had he not known? *Because it felt too good*. His brain ever-so-helpfully offered up images of Lucia, head thrown back in ecstasy. Her perfect tits on display for him. With amazing clarity of detail, he recalled everything from her scent, to her taste, to the softest patch of skin just behind her knee.

You took advantage. Had he? Fuck, had he hurt her? She'd been tight. *So damn tight*. She'd stiffened as he sank into her. In his defense though, she had begged him to keep going. She'd dug her fingernails into his flesh and raised her hips and—yeah—he'd kept going. He'd lost track of the number of times she'd come around his fingers, his tongue, his cock.

His dick twitched inside his jeans. *Down soldier*. No more of that. He had to figure out how the hell to apologize. That shit was never supposed to happen. One moment, she'd been so sad, hurting. The next, he'd been kissing her. And once he had his lips on hers, there was no going back. She'd given him everything, and like an asshole, he'd taken. And then left her. *You are a douche waffle.*

Shit, even Dylan gave him major side eye when he showed up to Lucia's apartment. There was no doubt in Noah's mind that he'd have a lot of groveling to do later. He cleared his throat. "Any movement?"

Dylan shook his head. "I relieved Oskar about an hour ago. Right now, she's got her best friend in there." Dylan shifted on his feet and slid his gaze away. "Honestly, dude, if I were you, I'd maybe leave me in my post for a while. Send Jonas, send anyone. But don't go in there alone."

Yeah, okay, he deserved that. He'd been a prick. She had every right to be pissed at him. And his men had a right to give him dirty looks. They all loved her too. *Wait, love?* No, he loved her like a sister. Then apparently he was from Hicksville, because that shit last night was far from sisterly.

There went his brain again, with all that helpful imagery. Lucia arching her body into his. Lucia calling his name. Lucia with her hands in his hair as he licked her. He wanted her again. Hell, he'd wanted her before he woke up this morning, with her body pressed tightly to his.

He wanted her now. Only difference was now, she very likely wasn't going to want him. Which was fine, because he didn't deserve to touch her anyway.

He took her virginity, and then he walked out on her. Who the hell did that? Something cold and slithery curled up in his gut. The real question was how the hell had he not known? All the signs were there. She'd looked worried, asked if she was doing things right.

And fuck, if he was being honest, he had pretty much ruined any chance she'd ever had at a real relationship. Usually before the guys got anywhere close enough to her to get her naked. And instead of some nice guy who was all gentle and kind, she'd gotten him for her first time. The way he'd touched her? How demanding he'd been? Yeah, he should kick his own ass.

"Thanks for the advice, but I got this." Noah nodded at Dylan then drew in a deep breath and pushed open the door to find JJ and Lucia on the couch, empty tubs of ice cream in front of them, and liquor. *Empty* bottles of liquor.

Oh shit. Things were going to get ugly, fast. He

needed to diffuse as quickly as he could. "Hey JJ, can I talk to Lucia for a minute?"

From the couch, JJ raised a brow. Then she said something to Lucia, who wouldn't even look at him. When JJ pushed herself up to full height and strode over to the door, Noah had no choice but to consider his weapon options. She was small, but he knew the look of murder in someone's eyes.

When she reached him, she placed her hands on her hips, legs akimbo. "You are a grade-A asshole. You know that? For years, I have encouraged her. Because like a fool, I believed you cared about her. But now? You've proven you're just like the other douchebags in the world. You hurt my best friend. You only live right now because I *allow* it. And I only allow it because she won't *let* me kill you. And that's only because she's afraid I'll go to jail." She chuckled. "Little does she know I'd be running the joint within a week."

His lips twitched. He wanted to smile. But he knew that was not the right response. JJ was taller than Lucia. All blond hair and big blue eyes. She was cute. He also completely believed that she could run any prison in this country. She radiated Valley girl cheerleader but was tough as nails. She didn't fuck around. Especially not when it came to her best friend and her feelings.

"JJ, if you just let me speak to Lucia —"

"No, asswipe. You do not get to speak to Lucia. Because not only did you abandon her after you two fucked like rabbits— my term, not hers—you put a goddamned armed guard at her door who won't let her leave. Asshole is calling it *detaining*. I call it kidnapping. Not sure, but it doesn't matter because all of this is against her will. Which means I'm about to call every lawyer in the city, and you are going to have your license for security, or whatever the hell it is that you do, revoked. Do I make myself clear?"

Noah was losing patience quickly. He needed to get Lucia on the same page right the fuck now. He didn't have time to explain to JJ how this was none of her goddamn business. *See, right there? That's what makes an asshole. Remember what Jonas said?*

Noah forced himself to take a deep breath and to use a gentle tone of voice. This wasn't JJ's fault. This was *his* fault. "What I'm trying to tell you is that I'd like to apologize to Lucia. An apology works better if I can be sincere and private."

JJ's brows popped up. And her lips formed a small *oh*. "Okay, fine. You can apologize or whatever. But I'll be waiting right here when you're done. If she finds it lacking in any way, your ass is mine."

She punctuated that last statement with a pointy-fingered jab to his chest. And while Noah knew he was bigger than her, he had a sudden fear for his balls.

"Lucia, can I see you in the bedroom please?" He didn't even wait for her, instead marching ahead straight to her room. He hoped she'd follow, because if not, he'd go out there and make her follow. *No. Remember, finesse*. The way he'd been doing things had gotten him where he was now.

The problem with meeting in the bedroom was that it still smelled faintly of sex. And of Lucia. Her perfume, her body oil, her shampoo. And there was still evidence of all the things he'd done to her last night, including the twisted, tangled sheets and comforter on the floor. She'd left the bedroom untouched from the morning, which was unusual. She usually liked things neat and tidy. She would've made the bed and changed the sheets. This wasn't her.

When she walked into the bedroom, her face was a placid mask showing zero emotion. "What do you want, Noah?"

He started to speak but then couldn't find the words, and his shoulders sagged. "Lucia, I would never have left you if I could've helped it. You have to know that."

She crossed her arms. "What I know is that I woke up and you were gone. That's not your fault. It's my fault. I don't know why, but somehow I trusted that you would be there when I woke up. I trusted that I wasn't just anyone in the legion of women you've slept with. You see, I'd convinced myself that last night was *something*. And that is my fault. Instead of waking up with me to pick up where we left off, or hell, just to do the grown-up, mature thing, you sent me Dylan. Which caused all kinds of feelings I can't even explain, but demoralizing comes to the top of my mind."

Noah strode right up to her. But she held her ground and tilted her chin up at him. "Lucia, I'm sorry.

That is not how I wanted everything to go down. Especially not for your first time." Noah frowned. "Why didn't you tell me?"

Lucia winced as if she'd been slapped. "You could tell?"

Fuck. And now she felt like shit because she thought he'd known all along she was a novice. He ran his hands through his hair. "No. I couldn't tell. Which is why I wasn't more —" He searched for the right words and finally settled on, "Gentle. If I'd known—" He stopped short and started again. "That's something you should tell a guy. I would've taken more time. Or *something*. Shit, I wasn't supposed to be your first, Lucia."

She glared at him. "Well, it's too late for that now, isn't it?"

"Why didn't you tell me?"

She rocked back on her heels, allowing her anger to give way to hurt for the first time. "Because you would have stopped. And I, like an idiot, thought you were what I wanted. But you're not."

Noah stared at her. She was lying. She may be pissed at him, but her pupils were dilated. And her nipples were tight. He could see them clearly through her thin T-shirt. He forced his eyes to hers. "No, sweetheart. You *do* want me. At least your body does. But I'm inclined to agree with you. Last night never should have happened."

"Oh that would be convenient for you wouldn't it, Noah? You were as much a part of last night as I was. You need to deal with me now. I'm not just Rafe's little sister anymore. You slept with me. You don't get to pretend it never happened."

"You think that's what I want? You're wrong." He leaned close, careful not to touch her. He kept his voice low and guttural. "What I want is to drag you back into that bed and rip that T-shirt off of your body because you should never be covered. I also want to bury myself so deep inside you that you don't walk again for a month." He forced himself to pull back. "But that's not what I'm going to do. Because right now there are bigger things at play. Your life is in danger. And not just some unknown, ephemeral danger either. I got a call from an old associate last night. Someone is trying to kill you. So until I can figure out who that is or what they want, you're keeping your armed guard. Sometimes two or three. I will put the whole damn firm on you if I have to, but I *will* keep you safe."

"You know, I'm so sick of you saying things like that to me. Rafe used to do that, too. Keep me safe from whom? Who is this old associate that you know? How do you know him? How is it that a guy who owns a security firm knows when someone's trying to kill me?"

"I can't answer those questions for you. You have to trust me."

"Trust you? After you walked out on me? Yeah, good luck with that."

Her scent filled his nostrils and made him dizzy. "You don't like me very much right now. And I understand why. Shit, *I* don't like myself right now. Considering I didn't have the pertinent information that I needed, I didn't know how badly this morning would affect you. All you need to know is that I didn't do it to reject you. I didn't do it because I didn't want you. I did it because I needed to get working on keeping you safe. If you don't like it, I get it. But the truth still stands. Someone's trying to hurt you, and I'm the only thing standing in their way. No way am I letting anything happen to you. Not on my watch. So for the time being, my guys stay on you like glue."

She was having none of it. "Oh yeah? Does that mean you too?"

"Of course. I'll be sticking closer than any of the others. I shouldn't have touched you. But it's too late for that now, because now that I have, I'm not stopping. So I'm going to stay close until you realize you want me to *keep* touching you. And while we're at it, you're not going to that fashion show thing."

Lucia gave him a wide smile and his balls shrank up inside of him. "That's super cute, Noah. But I'm going. And if you try to stop me, I will become the biggest pain in the ass you've ever met in your life. My job, my life, is important to me. You want to be the one who protects me. I might not be able to do anything about that, but I can make your life hell. So work fast to figure out who wants to hurt me, and follow me if you have to, but if you think I'm letting you come anywhere near me —"

He shouldn't have done it. He really shouldn't. But there was something about fighting with Lucia that made his blood burn. He dragged her to him and kissed her soundly on the mouth, letting all the frustration of this morning and the revelation that last night had been her first time pour into that kiss.

When he released her, she staggered backwards. "You make my life difficult—I can do the same. If your fashion show is so important, fine, you'll go. But with all of us in tow. I'll be back tonight. I'm on watch duty."

"Send Matthias." She called out after him.

As he turned the doorknob, Noah turned to look at her and gave her an evil grin. "Matthias isn't getting anywhere near you in your T-shirt and panties. I'm the only one who's going to be that close to you."

With that, Noah stormed out, leaving JJ on the couch with a confused look on her face. He barely grumbled a goodbye to Dylan as he left.

Noah hadn't been kidding about the extra detail. This morning, it was Jonas and Dylan. At noon, that had switched over to Ryan and Oskar. She had a feeling that tonight when she left the office, Matthias would be joining her in a private car. With this small team, there was no way he could keep this up forever.

So far they'd been discreet. They only stopped her from taking the subway like she usually did and insisted on driving her to work instead. To her chagrin, somehow each of them had managed to get a shift as a security guard at her building. So there was one guy upstairs on her floor by the main entrance. How Noah had gotten that approved by Adriana, she'd never know. And there was one guy guarding the front. She didn't know how they managed to pull that off either, and she wasn't going ask.

One day, if she ever decided she was talking to Noah again, she'd ask him. But for right now she was too irritated. Too pissed off.

Luckily, Adriana strolled by her desk and dropped off FedEx parcels to be taken downstairs. At least it gave her something mindless to do. With fashion week so close, much of Lucia's work was frantic and repetitive, and she felt like she was running in circles. She hated always feeling like she was behind, or would forget something. But this, taking packages down to messenger out, this she could do. Simple, mindless. And she didn't have to think about people trying to hurt her, or Noah, or the fact that she freaking missed him. Which was just wrong and unfair.

She nodded at Ryan when she passed the security barrier and made a left toward the FedEx window in the building. She wondered if she could even make it out the door without Ryan seeing her and notifying his partner. But there was no way. The front doors could easily be seen, and no one was getting upstairs without a pass. They'd probably tapped into the building's cameras, as well. Which was just damn perfect.

Lucia dropped off the packages and turned back

toward the stairs when she gasped. Someone was waiting just to the left, in the doorway. "Brent?" She shifted her glance over to the guard desk. While she had a clear view of Ryan, he couldn't necessarily see her that well. Or who she was talking to. "What are you doing here?"

Brent ran a hand through his hair. "Look, I've—I've been wanting to call."

She sagged. "I meant to call too. I'm so sorry about what happened with Noah. Just look at him like an over protective adopted brother or something. He's pretty much always an asshole. Even to me."

He nervously shifted on his feet. "Lucia look, I know when you came by the office and asked for information, you said you were looking for something to help someone in your family. And I wanted to help you. I did."

She frowned. "But you did help me." Not that she was going to use that information any more.

"That's just the thing. I gave you enough information that was true, but there's some falsified material in there, as well." He pulled an envelope from his coat. "This is the real information."

She glanced at the manila envelope. "I don't understand."

"I shouldn't be here giving this to you. But look, when I moved to the city, I was desperate. When I got that job at the records office, some guy offered to pay me a shit ton of money just to make sure that no one ever got their hands on these particular records, and I didn't think anything of it. Well, I did, but it seemed harmless at the time. And then you came looking. And I did what I was supposed to do; give you the wrong information and send you on your way. But I made the mistake of asking you out. You were just so pretty."

"What are you saying?"

He sighed. "I'm saying that I was paid to notify them if anyone ever came looking. The day you first came and asked, I notified them. But once I got to know you a little and we went out, I liked you. I can't lie to you anymore. You seemed really sincere about why you wanted the information. I'm not sure what you're looking for, but a couple of days ago I noticed some guys following me. So, this information must be important. I'm going to head out of town, but I didn't feel good about you not having what you needed."

"You're being followed?" She wondered if that was Noah's guys. But with such a small team, how could they possibly do their jobs, watch her, *and* follow Brent? Besides, it made no sense. "Brent look, if you'll just come with me…Noah— he's an asshole, but he'll help. This is important."

Brent shook his head. "No. I got myself into this mess, and I'm going to get myself out. Maybe head back home until things die down. I suggest you do the same thing. But I'm getting the hell out of here."

Her fingers traced over the lip of the envelope. She wanted to open it. She wanted answers. That part of her that was always searching, lingering at the edges of her nightmares she couldn't see, that was the part of her that needed to know the truth. *It's not safe. You need to stay safe.* Yeah, but what good was staying safe if she couldn't really live?

"Thank you for bringing me this."

Brent shook his head. "Look, I know you really need that information, but this whole thing is bigger than I knew. Just promise me one thing?"

She met his gaze and nodded. "Of course."

"Be careful. These are not the best guys to get tangled up with, so please, promise me. Even if you need to go to that Noah guy for help, I'll feel better leaving if I know you're safe." He hesitated then added, "I'm sorry."

Lucia watched as he hurried out the front doors. All the answers she wanted were right here in her hands. She just had to be brave enough to take that next step. *Are you ready to accept the danger?* She didn't care. Lucia was done with letting Noah protect her. She wanted resolution, and she was starting with this.

Chapter Thirteen

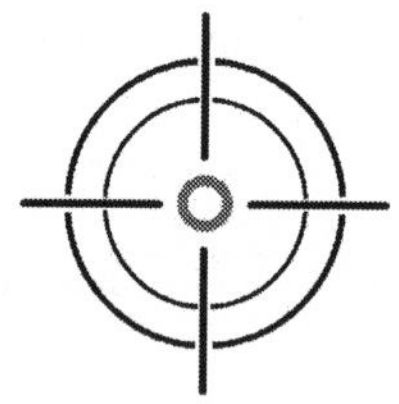

Noah took everything out of his pockets, including his wallet, keys and phone and placed them in the small plastic basin provided for valuables. Then after walking through the metal detectors, he claimed his things and waited for Matthias.

"Please be careful with that," Matthias protested as

the security guard put his headset in the basin. The guard, an older woman with her dark hair pulled back into a tight bun, waved him through impatiently. Matthias walked through the metal detectors and then had to double back when the alarms blared.

Noah rolled his eyes as Matthias was subjected to a pat down and then scanned with the handheld metal scanner. When she found another cellphone in his back pocket, the guard pursed her lips in annoyance.

"Sorry." Matthias grinned sheepishly.

She continued scanning his body and a few chirps erupted from the device as she passed over the front of his body. As she brought the scanner right in front of his crotch, it chirped again. Matthias turned bright red.

"Um, sorry?"

The guard pulled her hand back quickly but Noah caught the faint smile on her face as she turned away. Matthias gathered his stuff hurriedly and then jogged to catch up with Noah.

It wasn't nice to tease the man who held his entire electronic footprint in the palm of his hand but Noah couldn't resist.

"I never thought you'd turn out to be the security risk getting in here."

Matthias flushed again but laughed. "Sorry about that. It's a new…um…piercing."

"*Right*. It's always you nerdy types who turn out to be the real kinky bastards."

They were escorted to a small waiting room, and Noah sat gingerly in a hard blue chair facing a coffee table filled with magazines. The celebrity face staring back from the magazine cover wasn't familiar, although all the recent celebrities looked the same to him. He sighed. When had he gotten this old? Matthias walked over to one of the windows and looked out. After a few minutes, he paced back to where Noah was sitting. It was only when he could see the other man's face that Noah figured out the weird tension he'd picked up on.

Matthias was nervous.

"Hey, are you okay? If you don't want to do this then we can leave right now and I'll tell the Deputy Director of Whatever to fuck off."

Although this was potentially the most lucrative contract he'd ever been offered, Noah had more than a few reservations about getting in bed with the federal government himself.

Matthias shrugged. "It's fine. Just feels weird to be voluntarily meeting with law enforcement, you know?"

"Yeah. Believe me, I understand." Noah chuckled at the thought. He shared Matthias's distrust of all people in power, but for the first time, at least *he* was in control.

Despite his knee-jerk instinct to avoid all law enforcement, he wasn't really worried. There was nothing to worry *about*. When Rafe had taken him on as an apprentice, he'd assured Noah that there would never be any way to tie 'Steven Noah Williams' to his new identity of 'Noah Adam Blake.' His time working for ORUS had screwed him up in the head, maybe more so than he'd already been, but they took care of their people.

Their assets, he corrected himself. The shadows behind the ORUS curtain didn't care about any of them as people. They were tools to be used until they weren't useful anymore. Or until one of them gained the leverage needed to negotiate escape the way he had. The way he'd negotiated for Matthias.

It wasn't something that happened often.

A young woman appeared at his elbow. "Gentlemen? He's ready for you now."

Matthias glanced at him and nodded his head. The woman looked between them in confusion at the delay so Noah stood. They followed her down a long hallway and when they reached the last door, she stood aside to let them enter first.

The man behind the desk stood and came around with his hand outstretched.

"Thank you for coming on such short notice. John Calhoun. I'm the Deputy Director of the FBI's Cyber Division."

Noah shook his hand. "Noah Blake. This is my associate Matthias Weller. We understand you've had a few threats you can't trace recently."

While they chatted, Matthias remained standing, only nodding his head when appropriate. With every minute that passed he got more agitated, and Noah decided that they could do without the revenue from this contract.

From the day he'd pulled Matthias out of ORUS, he'd vowed to do for the kid the same thing Rafe had done for him. Teach him. Protect him. Show him that there was a better way. He hadn't come this far only to send him back into the lion's den before he was ready.

He glanced over at Matthias again. A fine sheen of sweat glistened on his forehead, and his fingers clenched the strap of his computer bag so tightly the skin was pulled white over the knuckles.

"Thank you for the meeting. I'll take everything back to my team and we'll devise a plan to see if we can tackle this."

Calhoun looked shocked, and Noah had to smother a laugh. He was willing to bet not too many people cut him off or interrupted his long-winded bullshit. Being the Deputy Director of anything in the FBI tended to gain people's respect. Most people's. Just not his.

"Of course. Of course. Let me know what resources you need."

Noah tuned him out again, focused on getting Matthias out of there. When he leaned over to shake hands with Calhoun again, his eyes were drawn to a picture on the desk. Before he had a chance to look closer, Matthias suddenly turned and walked out.

"We'll be in touch," Noah assured the director before following.

He found Matthias in the waiting room pacing back and forth in front of the receptionist's desk. Wild-eyed, Matthias turned to him, his jaw set like he was daring Noah to say anything. The kid should have known better because no one understood catching a case of the vapors around the cops like Noah did. After years on the streets trying to avoid detection, it was ingrained to avoid all law enforcement like you avoided STDs.

Something in his face must have broadcast his understanding because the tension left Matthias's shoulders. In that moment, he wasn't the brilliant killing machine Noah knew him to be. Instead he looked his age, young and vulnerable, and Noah didn't care if they lost the contract or not. Matthias hadn't had an easy life either, although Noah didn't know many details other than he'd escaped from England right before Scotland Yard could catch him with a rap sheet longer than an escort's contact list. But since the moment they'd met, he'd seen something in Matthias that reminded him of himself. Something worth saving. He would do whatever was necessary to get the kid the hell away from his personal bogeyman.

"Let's go."

Matthias didn't ask any questions, just followed Noah while muttering hasty goodbyes over his shoulder. Once they were out on the sidewalk, they moved quickly to the second level of the parking deck where they'd left the car. When they were on the road, Matthias looked over at him.

"Do you ever worry that your past will circle around and come back for you one day? That the stuff you did for ORUS will have consequences down the line?"

Noah sighed. "Every day."

Lucia was distracted all day and found herself making simple mistakes. She could only hope that she hadn't screwed up anything that Adriana would notice. But constantly looking over her shoulder had made it impossible to focus on the myriad ridiculous demands that she normally handled with aplomb.

Ordinarily, Lucia had a great sense of humor about her job. At least she was doing something she loved, right? But lately she'd started to wonder about the direction of her life. Brent's visit had only hammered the point home. He'd taken a great risk to do the right thing and let her know what was going on before he'd left town. There were a lot of people who wouldn't have bothered in his position. Who was she to him, really? Just some girl he'd gone on a terrible date with once. He didn't owe her anything at all.

At two o'clock, she gathered her things and stuck her head into JJ's cubicle to say goodbye. Even though she'd gotten approval to take off early from HR weeks ago, she was always strategic when she had plans to leave before her normal quitting time. It wouldn't be unheard of for Adriana to invent some task she wanted taken care of at the last minute.

"I'm off. Hopefully Adriana doesn't need anything while I'm gone but can you cover for me just in case?"

"Sure, no problem. Nonna's okay, right?"

"Yeah, she just has a doctor's appointment today. I like to take her to make sure I hear the doctor's instructions. Now that she's having all these problems with her blood pressure, I want to make sure she's doing what she's supposed to do. She's so stubborn sometimes."

"Wonder who that reminds me of," JJ muttered.

"Hey, I'm not stubborn. I just know what I want." She left JJ with a wave and took the stairs down to the first floor instead of waiting for the elevator.

It was nice to be out in the sunshine in the middle of the day but there was no time to waste. Nonna had an appointment at three thirty so Lucia had made sure to allow enough time to get to Queens even if the trains were running slowly.

As always Lucia had a shadow. Ryan this time. As annoying as it was, he gave her space so it was easy enough to forget he was there. Luckily the subway wasn't experiencing any delays for once, and Lucia arrived roughly thirty minutes later. She knocked once and then opened the door with her key. To Lucia's surprise, Nonna was in the living room working on the big book of crossword puzzles that she'd had forever. She was wearing the floral housecoat that she normally wore to bed.

"Hi, Nonna." Lucia offered her cheek for a quick kiss. "Did you forget that you have a doctor's appointment today?"

Her grandmother blinked. "I had my doctor's appointment last week. Everything is fine."

Lucia let her handbag drop to the floor with a thud. "Nonna! I took off work to take you."

"I'm sorry. I thought I'd mentioned to you that I'd already gone. I didn't want to worry you with my troubles. You're a busy career woman now."

Instantly Lucia felt terrible. She was having a crisis but she shouldn't take it out on Nonna. All these years she'd complained that her grandmother didn't take her career ambitions seriously, and now that she finally was trying, Lucia should appreciate it. She followed as Nonna got up and went into the kitchen. She watched as her grandmother put on a kettle for tea.

"You probably did. I've been distracted lately but that doesn't mean that I'm ever too busy for you. Well, what about the bill? I can still take care of that."

Nonna didn't look at her and suddenly got very busy cleaning a spot on the countertop. "It's fine, *amore mia*. You don't need to worry about any of that."

Lucia narrowed her eyes. Nonna only slipped into Italian when she was nervous or agitated. So that behavior, along with her uncharacteristic reluctance to talk about her doctor's visit, something she'd normally love to complain about, only made Lucia's suspicions grow.

Nonna was hiding something.

"Where's the invoice? I'm sure the insurance didn't cover everything. I'll pay the balance for you. It's really no problem."

Nonna looked up at her with a hesitant expression. "It's already paid for. I told you I save money for a rainy day."

The sound of the door opening drew both of their attention. Her grandmother bustled around the counter, strangely eager to investigate. Lucia followed her and they both stopped when they saw Noah standing in the entryway.

"Noah, what a nice surprise!" Nonna welcomed him with open arms and he leaned down obligingly to kiss her cheek.

"Sorry to interrupt, Nonna." Noah glanced over at Lucia. His eyes scanned her from head to toe as if looking for damage.

For a moment, Lucia forgot how angry she was as she took in his appearance. His eyes were wild and kept darting around like he expected something to pop out at him. Finally their eyes met, and the energy that crackled between them was palpable. Her heart flipped at the anguish she saw in his eyes. Something was very wrong.

She took a step toward him before she stopped herself. This was how he always drew her back in. He did something unacceptable, but then she'd look into those deep brown eyes and forget all about it. But that wasn't going to work this time. He'd crossed the line, and Lucia was done making excuses for him.

Lucia rolled her eyes and turned around, hoping her grandmother wouldn't pick up on the tension between them. Ever since Rafe's death, Nonna had accepted Noah as his surrogate in their family. She was from the old school, and while there were a million rules Lucia was expected to live by, Noah had carte blanche to pretty much do whatever he wanted. In Nonna's way of thinking he was the "head" of their family so she'd always turned a blind eye to his faults.

As much as she liked to believe she was a modern woman, Lucia had to admit she'd been guilty of doing the same. All these years, she'd accepted Noah's interference in her life. But those days were over.

"I'm going to go. There's so much work I need to catch up on. I'll see you later Nonna." Lucia kissed her grandmother quickly and then gathered her handbag from where she'd dropped it near the couch.

She could hear Noah making his excuses and then his footsteps on the concrete behind her as she walked down the sidewalk toward the subway. Normally she'd engage, start a fight, maybe even scream at him, but no more. He could follow her but he couldn't make her talk to him. It was time to stop entertaining his nonsense.

Chapter Fourteen

Lucia shivered in the cool air of the church, the dimly lit interior forcing her eyes to adjust. Stopping right in front of the holy water font, she gently dipped her finger in and crossed her forehead. She blanketed all of her emotions and feelings in a thick layer of numbness. She did not want to feel this way. She didn't want to feel anything. She didn't want her pain to rise to the surface and bubble over, spilling on everyone she loved. She didn't want it to affect Nonna, JJ, or even Noah. Despite how angry she was with him, if she didn't do something soon, she was going to combust.

Last night, she'd slept fitfully and agonized over the day to come. It was the anniversary of her brother's death, six long years since his murder. How fitting that last night she'd remembered more of that ill-fated day than ever before.

She could recall being happy at Coney Island, eating hot dogs and riding fair rides. She had consumed more funnel cake than any human being should. Her brother had teased her, laughed with her, and won prizes for her. It was a perfect day until everything changed.

She'd gone to the bathroom, and in the span of time it took to wash the powdered sugar from her fingertips, she had washed away weeks of a happy and lighthearted mood. From the moment she'd returned to his side, Rafe's demeanor had gone dark, dour, and desperate. He'd been frantic to leave, frantic to get somewhere else. He'd begun to talk so quickly that Lucia couldn't understand him.

He'd been full of anger and what looked a lot like fear. The whole time in the car, he'd apologized. Kept saying how sorry he was. She knew his worried look, firm brow, the restless tapping of his fingers on the steering wheel.

Rafe only fidgeted that way when he was nervous. He'd been worried about something and Lucia didn't like it. Something had been wrong. She remembered Rafe giving her a gun. The gunshots. Her brother going down. The weight of the gun in her hand as she pulled the trigger. But when she tried to remember the face of the man she shot…nothing. Nothing but a dark, empty hole in her heart and memory. It haunted her. From the moment she'd fired that gun, her next clearest memory was of herself wrapped in blankets the next morning.

She'd woken on the couch in excruciating pain, her muscles so cramped that she hadn't been able to move them. Then Nonna told her Rafe had died the day before.

Her grandmother hadn't told her what had happened or how she'd gotten home though. Months later, based on what others had asked her and what the Feds had told her family, she'd realized that her brother had taken her somewhere that warm summer afternoon and had then been shot.

The police had found her in the Hamptons, several miles from the location, huddled under a payphone that she had used to call for help. They'd found her frightened, shaken, and in shock, and they had taken her home. She'd been covered in blood.

Lucia crossed over to the vestibule where the lit candles were. All lit in prayer for the sick, the lost, for those not yet born. She automatically put her stick in the flames and picked a non-burning candle to light. She whispered a quick prayer to a God she wasn't sure she believed in anymore. At the very least, a God she could no longer trust. After all, he had taken her brother.

In her peripheral vision, she caught a glimpse of

Noah hovering in the doorway, shadows covering his face, as if he were afraid to step forward. *Yeah, he better be afraid.* She was still angry with him because of the things he'd kept from her and the interference in her life. And damn it, she could tell he was hiding something even now. The way he had been so frantic when he picked her up from Nonna's yesterday. Normally, she would have poked, prodded, and teased him until his mood improved. This time, their relationship hung in the balance. It was time for him to apologize, and she wasn't going to let it go until he did.

Nonna brushed her hand on Lucia's shoulder. Lucia could see her lips moving in silent prayer. She looked at her grandmother and Lucia knew she had been wrong. Wrong to let Rafe go, wrong to stop digging.

She had been trying to do what was right, to do what everyone had encouraged her to do daily. Nonna, Rafe, even the guys at Blake Security were always pestering her about her job, her love life, and her future. What did she want to do next? As if they were attempting to fill her life with so many things that she had no time to dig into Rafe's or what had happened to him. It would be wrong to let it go. It would haunt her forever until she found out the truth.

With her grandmother's hand on her shoulder, she turned her attention back to the candles.

"Go on, tell me, Lucia. What did he do now?"

Lucia turned to Nonna. "What do you mean?"

Her grandmother rolled her eyes. "I have been watching the two of you bicker and squabble since you were a kid. Normally, you argue, work it out, then minutes later you two are laughing like loons. This looks serious. Yesterday, today, the look in your eyes…it's not annoyance or irritation, it's hurt. You look hurt baby."

Lucia didn't want to get into it. Not here anyway. Not when her heart should be filled with questions about her brother, not when she should be focused on her fury at what happened.

"Just the usual, overprotective nonsense," she replied.

For a moment her grandmother was still, quiet, then she softly said, "You could do worse than him, Lucia. I know I've been pushing you to find a nice Italian boy. One who would take you on trips far from New York. One that would give you other things to think about like babies and travel. Take you to a vacation house in Hawaii. I've been wrong about that. Maybe Noah Blake is the kind of man you need."

Lucia turned to face her grandmother. "What are you talking about? I don't need Noah. I'm twenty-one years old. I don't need a man. I'm not trying to find love or settle down. This is my life; I'll figure it out."

Nonna nodded and squeezed her hand, "Well in that case, there are worse men to figure things out with. Besides, he's the kind of man who'll protect you." Nonna shook her head. "I used to think he had too many shadows, that he was too much like your brother. Now I realize he's exactly the kind of man you need. Nice Italian boys like Antonio won't know what to do when the real trouble comes calling. Noah is the thing that trouble fears. He's the kind of man that would give his life to protect yours. He's good for you, and the two of you need to work out whatever you've got going on."

Lucia turned back to the candles. "It's not that easy. You can't trust someone who does nothing but lie to you all the time."

Her grandmother's voice was soft when she spoke. "You can't always see it, but sometimes those lies are really there to protect you."

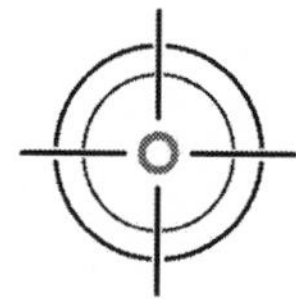

Noah stayed on the periphery of the entryway. He was neither inside, nor outside. Today being Sunday, most of the guys were off. But Noah had asked for a little extra help, just in case. Ryan and Dylan were out front; Ryan was posted at the front door. Dylan stayed in the car, watching the entrance, acting as surveillance.

Jonas was inside, sitting in the front corner, observing everyone that came in. Oskar was standing near the middle pew, his shrewd eyes watching everything, especially Lucia.

Noah was no stranger to Catholic mass. When Rafe was still alive, he'd occasionally dragged him along to Sunday mass with Lucia and Nonna. Noah hadn't minded so much back then, especially since a big Sunday dinner came with Sunday mass, and he'd been a growing boy with no family. So he'd figured he could survive church for a morning or two.

Even before then, he hadn't been completely unfamiliar with Catholic practices. A few of his foster parents had tried to incorporate the church into his life. The problem was just that he was bad to the core. None of the teachings had stuck.

As Noah shifted, standing just to the right of the holy water font, his eyes pinned on the one woman he shouldn't want.

Father Patrick Haney slid up to him. "Noah."

"Hey, Padre." He nodded.

"It's been a while since I've seen you here. You came more often when you were younger."

Noah rolled his shoulders. "The Padre" made him nervous. He worried that given his profession, the old man could see straight to his soul.

"Yes, well, that was before Rafe," Noah responded.

The Padre nodded silently. "Yes, but just remember, with or without Rafe here, your soul is up to you."

"There you go again, assuming I have one to save."

The father smiled, his cheeks pushing his eyes up until they crinkled into little slits. "Even the darkest of us have some good. Just like the best of us have some dark."

Noah watched as patron after patron walked up to the holy water and crossed themselves. One little boy pushed both his hands inside, then shook the water off. Noah swore that he felt a droplet hit his hand and it had warmed his skin. As if holy water knew who it was dealing with.

"Hey Padre, what does it mean when holy water burns your skin?" He stared down at his hand. "I'm, uh, asking for a friend."

Noah was only half-kidding, but the old priest turned his knowing eyes onto him. "It means you're being healed."

Noah could only watch in disbelief as the padre marched away from him to speak with Lucia and Nonna. *That old priest must be crazy*, he thought. Nothing was capable of healing Noah. He knew what he was.

What had happened at the FBI office yesterday had shaken him. He'd put Matthias in that situation, and it didn't sit well with him. He was supposed to be protecting the kid, not exposing him to threats.

Last night, Noah had tossed and turned on Lucia's couch as he dreaded today, the guilt eating at what was left of his conscience.

And of course the tension with Lucia was killing him. She still wasn't talking to him, and it made for sleepless nights and nightmares he couldn't shake.

Nightmares of an idealistic kid and the family that he had torn apart forever. No one knew the padre was 100% wrong. There was no healing for him. There was no redemption, only duty. Once Lucia was safe, he had to stay the hell away from her because everything he touched turned to ash.

Chapter Fifteen

The tension swirled around Noah and Lucia in the silence. What was he supposed to say? There was no answer that would work. Because at the end of the day he *was* lying to her. Had been for years. *What are you going to do when she finds out what you did?* He couldn't worry about that now. All he could do was keep her safe. Keep her protected. That was his job after all. What he'd vowed to do. Like he hadn't been able to do for Rafe.

Lighting candles for his friend seemed like the most hypocritical thing he'd ever done. *You are not the good guy*. Despite what the padre said, God didn't hear his prayers.

"You're really going to sit there and not say a word to me?" Lucia's voice was low, but had a razor sharp edge.

He deftly navigated the Manhattan streets heading back to her apartment. "Lucia, I don't know what you want me to say. There is nothing to say. I'm doing my job. I'm keeping you safe."

She turned to him. "You see, that's the problem. I never asked for your help. I never asked you to keep me safe. I never asked for any of this. All I ever wanted was a normal life. But no, my brother was gunned down, and I had to see that. Had to *watch* that. I see it in my dreams every night. And there is nothing I can do about it, just like there was nothing I could do about it then. When you say things like you're *protecting* me, that's a joke. Because you can't protect me from the real horror." She tapped her temple. "It lives in *here*. The nightmare of my own making."

Noah's gut twisted. "I can protect you. And I will. But I need you to stop. Stop asking questions. Stop poking. Stop digging. I need you to start listening to me because shit is about to get real."

"This is not a joke. You think I don't know shit is getting real? You have your goons following me everywhere I go. My grandmother is lying to me. *You* are lying to me. When do I get my life back?"

That was one lie he couldn't tell. Because if he lied to her now, the consequences would be dire later. "I don't know."

"You see? That answer isn't good enough. Your lies are not going to cut it anymore. I'm not some kid. I'm not fifteen. You guys think I don't notice. You think I don't notice that Nonna has all that unexplained money. Seriously, you think I'm dumb enough to believe that she's been squirreling that away all this time?"

"No one thinks you're dumb."

She continued as if he hadn't spoken. "I know there are times she went without things so that I could have something. She had that cash sitting there. She could afford a better place. But she stays there. She could travel more. I know it's always been her dream to see Italy. I thought she didn't have the money. I've been working hard to give back and she's lying to me. $5000 in a tin can in the back of her cabinet for a rainy day? That is a lie. It's been nothing but rainy days for a long damn time."

"Lucia —"

"No. Don't you sit there and lie to me. I know something is going on. Noah, you had *cameras* in my apartment. That explains so much now. How you always seem to know when I'm on a date. How you always come in just in time to keep me from doing things. You realize that's sick, right? You're like some crazy big brother stalker. You're worse than my grandmother. You think I don't know that you pay half my rent?"

He whipped his head around to stare at her. "What?"

"Yes, the super stopped me last week, and he said to tell you that the owners are upping the rent next month. And of course at the time, like an idiot, I thought he assumed you were my big brother or something, since you are the one asking all the questions about security and safety, and making changes to the apartment. Now I realize it's because you pay my rent. Damn it, Noah, I'm not a child. And it's time everyone stopped treating me like one."

"I'm not treating you like a child. I'm just trying to do what's right. If Rafe were here —"

"But he's not. And he hasn't been for a long time. Any obligation you had to my brother ended a long time ago. At some point, you have to let me live my life."

"You don't understand. Damn it, your life is in danger and you don't even know how much. And instead of helping me keep you safe, you're throwing a tantrum because I pay your rent. You want to put my balls in a vice because there are things that I don't tell you?"

"Noah, this is my life. Much as you would love to live it for me, you can't. How do you know my life is in danger? What's the plan? What are you going to do about it? This is usually the point when people call, I don't know, professionals like the police. I have a right to know."

As much as he wanted to, he couldn't tell her everything. As angry as she was with him right now, she would never speak to him again. It would forever change the way she looked at him. So he did what he did best; he deflected. "You know, I find it funny how you're all over me about keeping secrets when one of the most important secrets has been held by *you*. You used my stud services, and you left out one very important detail. The secrets I keep from you aren't selfish." *Liar*. "They are *for* your benefit. Every last one of them. They're not for me. The secret you kept…you held on to it for yourself. Because you knew I would have stopped."

Lucia stared at him. "Are you being serious right now? You somehow think this compares?"

He'd relieved Ryan of duty and taken over her watch after mass. He was still just as tense as he was yesterday. She watched as his grip tightened on the steering wheel. She could always tell when a point hit too close to home. "Lucia, this isn't a comparison, but this is a conversation we *can* have. One that doesn't put your life in more danger."

When they reached her apartment, he parked the car. He and Oskar pulled their typical watch pattern, one in front, one in back. Eyes open, always aware. Oskar took his post outside her door as Noah ushered her in. The placement of his hand on her lower back made her tingle. It also made her fume.

She turned on him. "Would you get your hands off of me?"

"Would you stop being so damn touchy? I was being polite."

"Polite? Like how you walked out on me? Was that polite?"

Noah threw up his hands. "Jesus fucking Christ. You seriously are never going to understand. I woke up, ready and willing to go another round. And then I got that goddamn call. The one that told me that the woman I spent half my life protecting was in danger. So I'm sorry if I couldn't crawl back in bed for a cuddle and a poke, but I had bigger things to deal with, like keeping you safe. I had to scramble to get someone here to watch you. And then I had to get back to the office so I could comb through your life and figure out who has the means and opportunity to hurt you. And then I had to start combing through *my* past, and Rafe's past. Because you've never done anything to anybody, so why anyone would want to hurt you is beyond me. I'm sorry that I couldn't be the kind of guy who brought you breakfast in bed, but you would think I could get some fucking credit for trying to do the right thing."

"You jackass. I wasn't asking for breakfast in bed. Shit, a text would've done. Something…anything so that I didn't have to wake up alone not knowing where you were or what happened. Or wondering if that was the worst sex you'd ever had in your life. But no, you let me wake up alone with Dylan at my door." Her breath heaved out of her chest, and the flush crept up her neck as she remembered the loneliness. The embarrassment.

Noah blinked. His lips parted and his brows furrowed in confusion. "Is that what you thought? Seriously?" He shook his head. "You saw me. I could barely move. I'm pretty sure you almost killed me. I have never felt like that before."

His words didn't compute because the emotion choked all blood flow to her synapses. Before she knew it, she was spilling her guts, emotion charging every word. "You promised you would always be here for me. Do you know what that's like? When the one person you're supposed to count on is gone after something like that? You've always been my constant, and then you ran like a coward."

"I didn't run. You have to know that it was not my choice to leave you. How can you not know how I feel?"

She felt that way? *Because you're an idiot*. Like a moron, he didn't even think to talk to her. To tell her. Give her any indication. *Instead you walked out. Shit*. Yes, he'd been reeling. He had never felt anything like that in his life. The fact that he felt that with Lucia, that shook him. He'd been her protector for so long.

Who was he kidding? She'd always been more than

someone to protect. Even when she was just a kid, he'd always gravitated toward being around her. How many other twenty-year-olds had fifteen-year-old kids for friends? She was smart, and sassy, and there was something so good about her. Something that he wished would rub off on him.

Even then, he'd hoped for some kind of redemption. He was good at what he did, too good. Someone like Lucia, a part of him had hoped that being near her could save him. And she had in a way. After Rafe, he'd known he had to protect her.

"You have to know, everything I've done, I've done to protect you. And I know that you don't believe me, but it's the truth." He shoved his hands in his pockets and rocked back on his heels. He sucked at this. He didn't do feelings. Feelings got you hurt. Feelings got you killed. *Like Rafe.*

"Noah, when are you going to see I'm not fifteen anymore? I don't need protecting."

The fury and self-hatred simmered under his skin. He stormed over to her, deliberately crowding her. He needed her to see what he was. "Do you know where I come from, Lucia? The things I've done? I can't even tell you. You would be so horrified it'd change how you look at me."

She blinked up at him and shook her head. "Noah, why do you think I was a virgin at twenty-one? Why do you think that I never managed to make it work with anyone?"

She wanted answers? Fine, he'd give them to her. "Because I've been interfering. I run off anyone who even gets close to you. What's worse, I lie to myself, and I tell myself that I'm protecting you. But really, I can't stand the idea of someone else with their hands on you."

She held his gaze. "Maybe some of that was you. But if any of those guys ever had a shot, they wouldn't have been easily run off. They would've stuck. They would've stayed. Risked an ass beating. But they *all* ran. And to be truthful, they were all your stand-in. For me, it's you. It's always been you."

Noah shook his head, but he couldn't bring himself to move away from her. "I don't deserve you." *But you want her.*

"Let me decide for myself."

Noah stared down into her gray eyes. *You're not good enough for her. You are going to get her killed. She deserves better. She deserves someone good. She wants you.*

Despite all the things that he knew about what was good for her and all the things he knew about that were dangerous for her, he couldn't stop. "Fuck it." Noah's arms snapped around her and drew her up close and he crashed his lips to hers.

Chapter Sixteen

Lucia held on to Noah's broad shoulders, trying desperately to keep pace with the kiss. Something seemed to have snapped inside of him, and the barrier that kept him so controlled was gone. His hands ran down her back and cupped her ass, kneading her soft flesh until she moaned into his mouth.

He wasn't being gentle, and heat flashed throughout her as he took what he wanted, bending her body to his will. When he lifted her off her feet, she wrapped her legs around his waist melting into him.

"You're the only one who has ever loved me," he whispered against her neck and Lucia stilled. Was he even aware of what he'd just admitted? Afraid to ask any questions and knock him out of the moment, she squeezed him tighter, hoping she could send her love through her skin to his. For all of his faults, he'd always wanted to take care of her. It had felt like being smothered at first, but maybe it was just because he didn't know how to love. By his own words he'd never had that kind of relationship before.

But she could show him. She could be his light in the darkness, his soft place to land, and the one he opened his heart to. That was everything she'd ever dreamed.

"I do love you, Noah. So much."

At her words, he shuddered and held her tighter. She pulled back slightly so she could see his face, and if her heart hadn't already been his, it would have been right then and there. There was such naked longing and hope reflected in his dark eyes. Had any man ever looked at her like she was as vital as oxygen? Noah stared at her like some fantastical thing that he couldn't believe was real.

"I love you, Noah." She said it again because he seemed to need to hear it.

His eyes closed and then he was kissing her

again, gentler this time, like she was the most precious thing he'd ever held.

"I'm the worst man you could have fallen for, but selfish bastard that I am, I'm not turning it down. You're mine now, Lucia. Do you understand that?"

His words would have sounded ominous coming from anyone else, but everything inside of her thrilled at the idea of belonging to Noah.

"You're mine, too. And nothing will ever change the way I feel about you."

His eyes darkened then, and he pressed a gentle kiss to her throat. "I'll be better. For you, I can be better."

Suddenly, he set her gently on her feet and then unbuttoned his shirt. Lucia watched with greedy eyes as he unbuckled his belt and pushed his slacks down leaving him in just his boxer briefs. Oh wow. She'd already been with him, but she couldn't get over how big he was.

Biting her bottom lip, she bent her arm under and pulled down the zipper of her dress, shimmying her hips until it pooled at her feet. Underneath she wore a plain black bra and panties, nothing special, but the way Noah sucked in his breath at the sight made her feel like a goddess.

"Make love to me, Noah. Just us, no secrets, no lies."

He knelt and picked her up, holding her against his chest as he strode down the hallway to her room.

Lucia giggled when he dropped her on the bed, spreading her arms to keep from bouncing all over the place. Noah smiled and then crawled over the bedspread toward her.

"I love that sound. All I ever want is to see you this happy, Lucia."

She ran a finger down his muscular chest and then circled his erection with her palm gently. His lashes drifted down on a strangled groan, and then he shot her a look that told her his erotic retribution would be swift.

"You have everything you need to keep me happy."

She stroked him gently and he groaned. "Fuck, princess, that feels so good."

Feeling bold, she slid her hand down his boxers and Noah cursed low even as his erection twitched in her hand. His hips pushed into her hand and he squeezed his eyes shut as he bit his bottom lip. She liked this kind of power. Liked how it felt to make him lose control.

When her fingertip found the bead of liquid and spread it over the tip of his erection, he shuddered but then quickly stilled her hands. "Princess, you have to stop. My control is already thin."

She frowned. "But I was exploring."

"I promise you, you can explore later. Right now, I want my mouth all over you."

He settled between her legs, his hard length rubbing against her panties in a way that made her shiver. His lips danced over her collarbone and then brushed over the stiff peaks of her nipples. She arched her back as the tingle of electricity shot straight to her core. While he wrapped his lips around her nipple and tugged, his other hand teased her free nipple, drawing it into a tight bud.

Lucia arched and bucked into each caress even as Noah whispered against her flesh. "You taste so good, princess." He slid his hand down over her ribs, to her hips, then to the juncture of her thighs. When his fingers moved the cotton to the side, she arched up trying to pull his fingers inside where she wanted them. Noah was happy to oblige, thrusting two fingers deep.

With a strangled curse, he pulled back long enough to yank her panties down her legs. Lucia sat up slightly, struggling to unhook her bra. There was nothing she wanted more than to feel his skin against hers. Noah reached behind her to assist and then threw the bra over his shoulder.

He looked down to where her legs had fallen open and his lips curled up briefly before he slid down and kissed the top of her mound. His tongue found her clit at the same time as his fingers found their way back home. Lucia moaned, and her head fell back at the dual sensations of being licked and penetrated.

"Always so wet for me," Noah murmured appreciatively.

Lucia didn't have time to be mortified by the comment because he added his thumb to the equation, circling and rubbing until all the energy in her body shattered into a million fragments of light and heat. He stayed with her as she bucked beneath him, his tongue lashing over and over, drawing every bit of sensation from her.

"Noah, please!"

All she could do was cling to his shoulders as waves of pleasure rolled through her, spreading from the top of her head down to the very tips of her toes. When she could finally open her eyes again, Noah was watching her with a look of dark satisfaction.

"Look at me, princess. I want to see your eyes."

As soon as their eyes met again, he climbed up her body and arranged her legs over his shoulders. Lucia gulped in air, trying to ready herself for him to take what he wanted. When Noah made love, he didn't hold anything back and she was so ready for it. He didn't seem to think that she could handle his deepest secrets, but she knew that no one else could ever accept him the way she could.

His hands settled on either side of her face. "I love you, Lucia."

She gasped at hearing those words for the first time and then again when he thrust deep. The position allowed her no room to hide and she felt tears well in the back of her eyes. Not from pain but from the stark intimacy of taking him this way, looking deeply in his eyes, accepting everything he had to give.

"I love you. I love you. I love you." He whispered it over and over as he took her hard, like he was afraid that if he didn't say it enough that it wasn't real.

But that had been Noah's only exposure to love, hadn't it? Something that didn't last, something that could be taken away from you at any moment. Tenderness swelled inside for this gentle giant of a man who was so afraid to love but had so much of it to give. Lucia's orgasm broke and she sobbed against his shoulder at the intensity of it.

Noah stilled and she felt him shuddering as his own pleasure took over. She wrapped her arms around him, never wanting to let go of what they'd found together.

For years, Lucia had dreamed about this, making love to him with no reservations. Now it was here and she could hardly believe this was her life. That she could touch him, kiss him, and hold him whenever she wanted, seemed too good to be true. But maybe the universe was done torturing her and she was finally going to get her happy ending.

A shot rang out.

Lucia moaned and tossed her head back and

forth. She didn't want to see what happened next. For the first time, she was aware that she was dreaming but could do nothing to stop the horrible images from unfolding before her. Lucia sobbed silently as she watched Rafe rummage through the glove compartment of his car, knowing what was coming next.

"Stay here. No matter what, okay?"

In her dream, Lucia smiled. She remembered thinking that her brother was always so worried about everything and that he really needed to learn to relax.

"Okay, fine. But really, where am I going to go?"

"I'm serious, Lulu."

Rafe pressed a gun into her palm and Lucia gasped. She'd never held a gun before, and the cold metal seemed so heavy in her hand.

"Take this. If something happens... you drive out of here as fast as you can."

"Rafe, I can't drive yet."

"I've taught you enough. Just drive, Lu. As fast as you can."

A shot rang out.

Lucia tossed her head and whimpered.

"Rafe!"

She wanted to protect him, to hold him close but where his body was supposed to be, there was nothing but blood. It flowed around her in rivers that threatened to sweep her away. She raised the gun and fired.

"I love you. Come back," she sobbed, looking

around desperately for her brother's body but it was too late. He was gone.

A shot rang out.

Suddenly, she saw the events happen with crystal clear precision, something that had never happened before. The man who'd shot her brother stood right in front of her, and she could see his profile clearly. Tall, dark hair, and so handsome. She'd come to love him over the past few years as much as she loved Rafe. Suddenly, his face morphed from a blur into Noah's face.

Lucia trembled in her dream, watching as the shot rang out and Noah jerked. She'd shot him. The shock of it was so horrifying that she woke up with a scream on her lips.

She turned her face into her pillow and sucked in a desperate breath. Noah slept next to her unaware, and she calmed herself by concentrating on the idea that dreams were just her mind's way of coping with the tragedy. It was just so strange for her mind to torment her by replacing the things she couldn't remember with Noah's face. Was it because of the recent changes in their relationship? Was she feeling guilty for moving on with Noah instead of searching for her brother's killer?

The explanation actually made sense and helped to slow her racing heart. Maybe it was time to listen to Nonna for once and go back to the therapist she'd seen right after Rafe's death. If she was ever going to move on and live her life, she had to come to terms with things. It wasn't abandoning her brother to want a normal relationship with a man who loved her. She was finally on the verge of getting everything she'd ever wanted, and she didn't want to let her fear hold her back.

Noah shifted slightly, and she could tell when he woke up because he stiffened, probably unused to having someone in bed with him. He'd confessed once, after she'd teased him about being a ladies man, that he'd never shared a bed overnight with anyone.

"What's wrong?" he whispered.

"Nothing. Just a bad dream. Sorry I woke you."

"Come here, princess." He held out his arm.

Determined to move past the horror of the nightmare, she curled up against him, resting her head on his chest. The solid beat of his heart lulled her until she could breathe easily again.

"Better?"

"Yeah. I'm glad you're here, Noah." She knew he didn't relax easily and knew what a big deal it was for him to spend the night with her.

"I'll always be here for you, Lucia. No matter what."

Completely content, she closed her eyes and ran her hand over the muscular planes of his chest. He was so beautifully made, and she took her time tracing the dips and curves of his abs, working up over the flat muscles of his pecs and the sharp points of his collarbone. Her fingers skimmed over a mass of rough flesh on his shoulder. Lucia's brow furrowed as her fingers dipped into the hard knot of skin. It almost felt like…a bullet wound.

She swallowed the sudden sense of unease. Noah was always chasing bad guys; of course he'd probably have bullet wounds. But her fingers kept tracing the skin over and over, and suddenly she was slammed with another image from her dream.

Her own hand holding the gun and then the kick of the weapon as she'd pulled the trigger. She watched as Noah jerked and his hand flew up to cover the wound on his shoulder. Their eyes met, and she'd seen the fear, shame, and guilt in his eyes.

Lucia sat up slowly, horror turning her blood to ice as she stared down at Noah's chest, fully illuminated by the moonlight coming through the window. She touched the scar again, and then Noah turned to look at her.

"It was you."

**The Shameless Trilogy continues with *Shameful*, to be released on 6/5/17

Coming soon

I am the thing that goes bump in the night. I am a liar, a protector...a killer...I am Noah Blake.

And now that she knows my secret, she hates me.

The guilt and shame I carry around is bad enough...But seeing the distrust in her eyes, that will kill me before my enemies do...

EXCERPT of *Shameful* (subject to change after publication)

Noah led the way into Lucia's apartment building. As she scowled at him, he bit back irritation and pushed down his guilt. After all, she had a point. She had every reason to hate him. Noah just wished it didn't hurt so much.

Anytime she glared at him or purposely avoided his touch, he was reminded of what he was. *Who* he was. There was no changing that now. All he could do was try and keep her safe. He'd been foolish to wish for more. Completely insane to think that she could love him.

Immediately the hair on the back of Noah's neck stood up. Something was off. The camera he had placed directly in front of the elevator was turned to the side as if someone had very deliberately pointed it that way. He put a hand on Lucia's elbow to stop her. She glared down at it.

"Can you relax? Stay behind me, be quiet, and take off those damn shoes."

"Why would I take off my shoes?" she hissed.

He shot her a glance as he pulled his gun out of his holster. "Because you can't run in those heels."

Her eyes widened, but she did what she was told. She shoved them into her purse and then cleverly slung her purse across her body.

Smart girl. She'd be able to move quicker that way.

He had to fight the urge to run, the urgency to get her to the safety of her apartment. Instead, he deliberately slowed the pace. As they turned the corner, he noted the other camera next to the stairwell. It was also turned up.

Why the hell hadn't Ryan reported that?

It wasn't until they rounded the next corner to the

right that he saw why. Ryan was slumped forward in his seat next to Lucia's door. Either asleep—or worse. And from the looks of it, it seemed much, much worse. Like he'd been bent and broken and put like that.

Lucia took one look at Ryan and ignored Noah's warnings. She tried to sprint ahead but Noah reached out and grabbed her wrist, halting her. He shook his head.

"But he's hurt!"

"Look at him, Lucia. Can you see his face?"

"No."

"So, how do you know it's him?"

Her beautiful face twisted with worry, then she did exactly as he wanted and shifted behind him. Noah approached cautiously. As they got closer, he saw the ring that Ryan wore on his middle finger. It was simple and silver. Noah was one of the few people who knew the ring's significance. Ryan never took it off.

Noah crouched beside the kid, checking his pulse. There was one, but weak. He'd been knocked out. He lifted his plain black shades and saw the contusions around Ryan's eye. To top it all off, blood was running out of Ryan's nose onto his dark suit. Lucia handed him several napkins and Noah did what he could to plug the leak. Then he noticed Lucia's door was ajar.

"I need you to stay here." He bent to his ankle holster and gave Lucia a gun. "Can you use this?"

She tilted her head and glared up at him. "You have a scar on your shoulder that proves I can."

Noah gritted his teeth. "Point-and-shoot at anyone

that comes out of that door that isn't me. Hell, if you have to, shoot me too. Just make sure you put holes in whoever it is. While you're waiting, call Matthias and send out an S.O.S. We're going to need some transport. I won't be able to carry Ryan all the way back to my car. They're better off picking us up out front. Watch your back. Do you understand?"

She nodded. Even as she swallowed hard, he saw her lift her jaw and square her shoulders. She was scared but she wasn't crumbling. She didn't ask inane questions, scream, or worse, cry. His respect for her shot through the roof. But he didn't have time to think about that. Without sparing her a second glance, he slipped into her apartment.

It was dark, but there was someone here. Noah could *feel* him. He couldn't explain it, but he knew he wasn't alone in the apartment. The real question was, where was this asshole?

He didn't have to wait long for an answer, because the moment he stepped into Lucia's living room, something shifted on his left. Noah narrowly missed being hit by one of Lucia's Dana Decker candles. Suddenly the intruder crashed it into the left wall of the kitchen, leaving a dent in the drywall as he tried to brain Noah with it.

Noah wasted no time, rotating on the ball of his foot and throwing a punch that landed with satisfying efficiency. *Crunch*. Instead of crouching, howling, or even muttering a curse word, the fucker remained silent. His head snapped backward then slid back into place as if Noah hadn't even landed one. This was no average burglar; this guy was a pro.

They circled each other in the living room like caged lions seeking a time advantage. Then it was on. His assailant applied a series of roundhouse kicks, and Noah caught one to the ribs.

Shit. That hurt, though it was probably not broken. He kept his vision on the guy.

The intruder was nearly his height. Being several inches over six feet, Noah was used to towering over most people, but this guy was just as big so the advantage of his reach was nullified. For anything truly worthwhile, Noah had to get up close and way too personal for comfort.

Throwing a series of combination kicks and punches and having only one or two land, he ducked the kicks and throws sent his way. He fought for Lucia. No way was he letting this guy hurt her.

Noah took one step in and came up with his right elbow, hitting the guy's chin. This one was the hardest punch of all, landing the unwelcome guest on Lucia's end tables, covering him in shards of broken wood.

Noah pressed his advantage as his assailant lay on the floor. Even as he approached, the guy had his head up, swiveling, following Noah's movements. As Noah approached, the guy shoved out a kick that landed high on Noah's thigh. The move was familiar to him as if the other fighter wanted to injure him, but not kill him.

The move was practiced and skilled enough that Noah knew he would be sporting a bruise for the next week or so. Although, the guy hadn't hit him in the knee. Noah would have never recovered from something like that.

Noah didn't have the same compulsion to preserve the other guy's life. He was here to hurt Lucia, which meant Noah had no qualms about killing him. He grabbed his foot, and the assailant kicked with the foot in Noah's hand while sweeping Noah off his feet with the other one. Noah had no choice; he landed on his ass but was back up in a second, as was his assailant.

They were like mirror images of each other. As one pushed his hands to the left, the other pushed his hands to the right.

This guy seemed to have had karate or jujitsu training. Given his kicks, tae kwon do, too. For what felt like another hour but was most likely mere minutes, they exchanged elbows and fists as they grappled, both trying to get the other to the ground to submit.

Hell, this is almost fun. All Noah wanted in the end was to pull the mask off.

If this guy was ORUS, that explained why he was trying to preserve Noah's life.

"You don't have to do this. Just leave."

The guy landed an elbow that jarred Noah so hard he could hear his teeth rattling in his mouth. That was all that was needed to roll him onto his back with an arm bar across his neck. Noah turned his head to alleviate the pressure on his trachea, but all the while, he threw punches. Planting his heels, he tried to use his hips to buck the jackhole off of him.

But suddenly there was a crash, and the guy was no longer raining fists on his face. He was trying to shake something off of the back of his neck. Noah risked injury to his trachea and turned his head. And sheer horror slashed through him.

Lucia.

Why the hell can't she ever listen?

Even though he was pissed at her, Noah still used her distraction to his advantage. As she tried to wrap her arm around the other guy's neck, he used the opportunity to land hard fists in his face. That was all the advantage he needed. With Lucia choking the guy from behind and him using the leverage to push the dude off and jump back to his feet, they had him dead to rights. But then the guy twisted, shoving Lucia backward onto the couch. She landed with a hard bounce and a curse. The guy turned his attention back to Noah and pulled him in with two hands around the back of his neck. Noah knew he intended to hit him straight in the gut. He knew where that knee was going. But instead of using his knee, the guy extended his foot, and sent it straight for the family jewels.

Mother. Fucker.

Brutal, sharp, electrifying pain took over Noah's world. Bright lights shone behind his eyes, and he struggled to keep it together. Scrambling for his discarded weapon on the floor, he fired, grateful he'd thought to put on the silencer.

The guy darted glances between Noah and Lucia, attempted to go for her, but Noah wasn't having that and he raised the gun again. Instead of going out the front door as Noah would've assumed, the guy jumped directly out of the open living room window. *What the—* Noah scrambled to his knees, his balls screaming at him to stop whatever the fuck he was doing and just lie down.

He was used to pain. What he was feeling now was nothing in comparison to what he would feel if he lost her. He forced himself to stand and staggered to the window. He looked around first but saw nothing. It was only when he looked straight down that he saw the guy clinging to a rope, rappelling down. So he'd had a plan for escape. He had likely been here earlier setting up that hook, planning his escape.

But why mess with the cameras? And when? Fuck, unless he'd been there before scouting. It was probably because he knew he would have to take out whoever was outside. There's no way the security alarm wouldn't have gone off and no way Ryan wouldn't have heard him rumbling around in here.

Ian was right. Someone was trying to hurt her.

Lucia ran to him. "Noah, oh my God. Are you okay?"

He wanted to lean into her caress, wanted to wrap her in his arms and hold her there, never letting her go, but he couldn't. It was too dangerous.

"What part of stay outside and guard Ryan did you not understand? Everyone has a job. I gave you yours. Next time, don't come in."

She stared up at him, bottom lip quivering. "I just saved your ass."

"You had a job. You failed it. What if he had a

second guy out there and Ryan's dead now?"

Horror crossed her expression and she glanced toward the door. "Oh my God. I just heard the fight in here. And I wanted to—"

"You have three minutes. Grab anything you think you'll need for at least the next two weeks. It's time to go. We're going to my place. We've already been here too long."

He didn't want to hear her apologize. He didn't want to hear her say that she worried about him, because those words would soften his stance. Being soft, caring about her too much, would get them both killed.

** *Shameful* will be available 6/5/17

ABOUT THE AUTHORS

New York Times & USA TODAY Bestselling author **M. MALONE** lives in the Washington, D.C. metro area with her three favorite guys: her husband and their two sons. She holds a Master's degree in Business from a prestigious college that would no doubt be scandalized at how she's using her expensive education.

Independently published, she has sold more than 1/2 million ebooks in her two series THE ALEXANDERS and BLUE-COLLAR BILLIONAIRES. Since starting her indie journey in 2011 with the runaway bestselling novella "Teasing Trent", her work has appeared on the New York Times and USA Today bestseller lists more than a dozen times.

She's now a full-time writer and spends 99.8% of her time in her pajamas.

mmalonebooks.com/malonesquared

USA Today Bestselling Author, **NANA MALONE**'s love of all things romance and adventure started with a tattered romantic suspense she borrowed from her cousin on a sultry summer afternoon in Ghana at a precocious thirteen. She's been in love with kick butt heroines ever since.

With her overactive imagination, and channeling her inner Buffy, it was only a matter a time before she started creating her own characters. Waiting for her chance at a job as a ninja assassin, Nana, meantime works out her drama, passion and sass with fictional characters every bit as sassy and kick butt as she thinks she is.

nanamaloneromance.net/malonesquared

Made in the USA
Middletown, DE
18 September 2017